Freshly Served

Chapter One

Alfie

"You signed me up for *what*?"

This had to be a joke. Earlier that day, I'd had a call from a producer of a TV show. Or rather, my agent had and they'd suggested the producer call me directly. That in its own right was probably a good indication of how excited I was by this opportunity.

It had taken me three separate times of the guy repeating himself before I even understood what he was saying. Apparently, I had signed up to enter a reality TV competition. Not just any reality TV competition, oh no. I had signed up to be on *Serves You Right*.

Serves You Right was a new show, the producer had explained to me after realizing that I wasn't joking around and honestly had no idea what he was talking about. It was a mix of a cooking show and one of those 'paired up with a celebrity' shows. Thankfully, no dancing was involved.

Or, well, maybe this was worse.

This involved cooking and I was, somewhat notoriously, terrible at cooking.

That was how I knew that someone on the team had done this. It was next-level chirping, I had to give them that, but it was still ridiculous. I couldn't go on TV and be terrible at cooking.

"Alfie Reeves, the TV star!" Felix shouted across the locker room like that helped anything. Some of the other guys laughed, which just made me roll my eyes harder.

"No, seriously, which one of you assholes did this? I'm not going to go on the TV and look like a dick trying to cook food." And I would definitely look bad if I did try, because I couldn't cook. Like at all.

"Hey, hey, but it's for a good cause, no? I thought that the money goes to some sort of charity?" Will asked.

Half of the money did, the producer had told me as much. Meals for kids from disadvantaged families. It was like a punch to the gut when I thought about saying that I couldn't do that.

The rest of the reward went to the person I would be paired up with. On top of that, they would pay me to be involved and, if I won, my share would be donated to support local children. How was I meant to refuse that?

"But I can't cook," I protested, feeling like there was a great chance I'd lose this argument.

Judging by the guys' expressions, they weren't very sympathetic to my plea. Part of me wanted to ask them how they would feel, if I signed them up to do something they were bad at on national television.

"Surely you don't have to be able to cook?" Chase pointed out. "I mean, that's why they pair you up with an actual chef."

Luke nodded, trying to hide a flicker of a grin behind his serious captain's expression. "Maybe you'll learn something," he said, tone utterly deadpan.

I snorted. Just because Luke had learned something from getting together with El, our nutritionist, that didn't mean that it was going to be the same for me. If lessons in cooking had been something I wanted, I could have arranged them on my own.

"I just don't want to look like a moron on the TV," I whined.

"I mean, it wouldn't be any different than how you look anyway, Alfie. Just on the TV," Olle informed me and, unlike Luke, he didn't even pretend to be hiding a grin.

Giving a dramatic sigh, I sat down on the bench. "So which one of you was it? Which one of you should I get a bag of dog shit for Christmas?" Maybe while I plotted my revenge, I would also figure out a way to get out of this. What was a good way to get out of potentially funding meals for needy kids?

The silence after my words fell like a weight, pressing down onto my shoulders. But nobody else seemed bothered, exchanging glances which made it perfectly clear they weren't going to tell me who was responsible.

Which made sense - if I didn't know which of them to blame, I couldn't take it out on any one person. So I'd just have to be annoyed at all of them.

"You really think you're going to look like more of a moron than whoever else they get on?" Will asked. "Why? It's not like they're going to pick celebrities who are already great at cooking."

There was a difference between 'not great at cooking' and me, and literally everyone on the team knew it. But I was hardly going to volunteer that particular information, not when it'd just lead to more chirping.

"Why would you even want me to do this?" I asked. Not that that was a serious question. If this was anyone else on the team, I would definitely be pushing for them to go on the show. It would be hilarious. Except now that it was me, it felt a lot less funny.

Chase shrugged, leaning back against his locker. "Why not?" He said it so casually that it was almost impossible to argue with. The only reason I didn't want to do it was because I would look stupid. But lots of hockey players had done reality shows, it wasn't as if I would be the first.

"It's good PR," Luke added. "And it's only six weeks, so it won't take up too much time. It's not like those dancing shows where you have to practice for hours and hours."

Everyone on the team knew better than to sign up for something which would cut into the Pumas' training time.

"It kind of sounds like I have no choice," I whined, making several of the guys laugh.

"You'll do great," Olle assured me, but I gave our goalie a suspicious look. He was much harder to read than the other guys, but somehow I got the impression that, just like the rest of them, he found this amusing. And really, it was hard to even blame them.

It was funny.

Just not to me, because it was about me.

"I guess I'm going on a cooking show," I sighed, my frown so deep it almost hurt.

There was a round of cheers, some of the guys coming over to thump my back - presumably in appreciation that I knew how to take a joke. Even if I was going to keep whining about it.

"Don't worry," Will said, barely managing to conceal a grin. "If you're really as bad as you think, you'll only have to do one week."

I didn't know whether that was more comforting or humiliating.

If I had to go on a cooking show, I didn't want to lose. I was much too competitive for that. Not to mention, the guys would never let me forget it.

"So this is really happening," I sighed dramatically.

After that, it was a bit of a blur of activity with me messaging my agent who got the ball rolling, so to speak. I had a bunch of contracts come through, all of which I was advised to read. It felt like it took forever to go over all the minute details.

I found out that the show would be filmed once a week, about five days before it aired. It seemed like a quick turnaround but who was I to know how reality TV was made?

There was a confidentiality clause, which made sense, even if I thought it'd be super hard not to tell the team how I'd done. But as Will had pointed out, maybe I'd go out in the first week, then it wouldn't be too much to hide.

Another clause informed me that I wasn't allowed to have an 'intimate relationship' with anyone on the show to ensure there were no accusations of favoritism or sexual harassment. It made me wonder how often that happened if they had to threaten people with disqualification.

With nothing else particularly standing out, I signed the contract. It had a kind of finality to it, like I was most likely making a huge mistake. But it was too late now. Or well, once I'd posted the contract off, anyway.

A few days later, things started really happening. Once I had triple-checked to make sure that none of the filming would interrupt any of my training or games, I was ready to be on TV. Well, as ready as I would ever be.

This still didn't seem like something I wanted to do but it was definitely too late to back out.

I had learned more about what the structure would be. I would be paired up with someone who worked as a chef or worked in catering. I wasn't really sure what the difference was, but whatever it was it meant that, unlike me, they would know how to cook. The winner would receive an investment toward starting their own business, which did sound like a pretty sweet prize.

On the first day, before the filming started, we were all introduced. I recognized only one of the other 'celebrities', a guy who had done some charity event with the Pumas. He was an actor but I couldn't think of anything I had seen him in.

There were another actor and a comedian. Also, a singer and someone who was off another reality TV show. I was kind of glad that they introduced us to each other, because I wouldn't have known who was a celebrity and who was... not a celebrity.

"So, can you cook?" I asked the guy I recognized, James. Hopefully, quietly enough not to get judgy looks from anyone else in the room.

He gave me a look I recognized, the same one that I got any time I admitted that, as a grown adult, I still couldn't make anything that actually tasted good.

"Some," James answered, making my heart sink. "I mean, I'm sure I can't cook as well as the professionals." He waved a hand towards the other side of the room, where a group of people in white aprons had started lining up against the wall.

There was a nearly even split of men and women, and at least one of them looked almost as nervous as I felt. I tried to catch her eye, thinking a small smile might reassure her that we 'celebrities' were nothing to be scared of, but she was looking anywhere but at me.

"But that's what they're here for, right?" James asked. "To tell us what to do and what will give us the best chance of winning."

Right. I did like winning. I just truly didn't think there was a chance in hell I would. It made me feel a little guilty as I glanced at the professionals. It wasn't whoever's fault that I couldn't cook; I would definitely put them at a disadvantage.

Looking at the professionals, it was easy to promise myself that I'd at least try my best. If there was one thing I could do well, it was to take instruction, so maybe that would have to be what my forte would be. God knew it wasn't going to be cooking.

"I hope I get paired with the hot one," James informed me, making me snap out of my thoughts and turn back to him.

"Well, isn't that a douche thing to say?" I frowned and he shrugged like it just didn't bother him.

"Hey, it's six weeks, got to keep myself entertained somehow." Except I was definitely now going to hope that James wouldn't last the whole six weeks. In fact, it would probably feel amazing if I managed to kick him off the competition.

Suddenly, my competitive nature was parading in full swing and we hadn't even been paired up yet. Thankfully, the producers announced that we'd start with the intro. They wanted to film us meeting and greeting each other, so I made sure to stand close to anyone but James.

"You play for the Pumas, right?" a woman asked from my other side. "I mean, when you're not competing on reality TV." That made me laugh, and I confirmed that, yes, usually I was a lot more comfortable on the ice than anywhere else.

"Yeah," my companion agreed, introducing herself as Maxine. "This whole thing is really far outside my comfort zone." It was reassuring to know that not everyone felt as secure in the competition as James did. But I doubted Maxine would be as hopeless as I was.

Before I could say as much, Maxine glanced towards the professionals. "I just hope they picked chefs who are good at working with beginners."

"Me, too," I agreed with a nod. This was already a much better start, someone else who didn't feel too confident. "You're a singer, right? I guess this is pretty different." Well, not really any more different than what I was used to. Hockey, I could do. Cooking... not so much. At least, unlike Maxine, I had the competitiveness down.

Maxine hadn't gotten much further than 'I am' before the producers were calling us to get into our places.

"We're going to get a couple of shots of this, so if things feel like they're repeating, do your best to pretend they're not."

And we were off.

I'd done interviews for the Pumas, but this was all very different. There were lights and cameras everywhere, it was a bit difficult to figure what to focus on first.

"Can you not stare into the camera, please?" someone called and I had no idea if that was to me or someone else, but I made sure to look away. They started introducing the different professionals and at least it was easy enough to focus on that, since I was genuinely curious who was who and what they did.

The woman whose eye I'd tried to catch earlier was introduced as Christine, a chef at some fancy restaurant in Salt Lake that I'd never been to. She tripped over her words as she tried to talk about what a great opportunity it was to be on the show; they had to take her all the way back to the beginning to film it again.

Christine apologized, adding that the cameras were pretty unnerving. In a way, it seemed to make everyone else feel a little better. Maybe it wouldn't be so embarrassing if we screwed up now that someone else had already done it first.

Once they'd managed to get a clean take, Christine was paired up with Tex, the reality TV star.

"James, you're next," the producer called, swiveling the camera to face him.

I felt a little sorry for whoever got paired with James. Sure, we'd only talked for about half a minute, but he didn't seem like someone I would want to be paired up with. It wasn't particularly hard to figure out who 'the hot one' he'd referred to was. One of the women definitely stood out.

She was probably the youngest of the professionals, maybe mid-twenties, like me. Her brown hair seemed to frame her face perfectly and it took me a moment to realize that it probably genuinely did. The show had hairdressers to make our hair camera ready, which was pretty cool.

Unlike Charlotte, the brunette met my eyes straight on and I could practically feel my heart skip a beat. It must have just been nerves, I was sure. Looking away, almost feeling like I'd been caught in the act, I focused on seeing who James was going to be matched up with.

It wasn't her. That made me give a soft sigh of relief.

Instead, James was matched up with one of the men - Aaron. He was older and I felt like maybe that'd be good, someone who would face James' douchiness straight on. Not that I didn't think the brunette could have! It just seemed easier not to.

After James, a Youtuber I had also never heard of called Legacy was paired with a woman who looked like someone's grandmother, called Renata. She seemed lovely and Legacy looked like he'd never been close to a grandmother, so that was going to be fun.

With only four of us left to be matched, we all eyed each other up. There didn't seem to be a predictable structure to how this was done, so it surprised me that I turned out to be next.

"Alfie, our NHL star," the host - Alix - introduced and I tried very hard not to blush. It wasn't untrue, but it still felt kind of weird to be introduced as a *star*.

In my efforts not to look directly at the camera, I found my gaze returning to the brunette. Once again, she met my eyes, giving me a smile that looked almost as teasing as it was reassuring.

"Alfie, you're going to be cooking with Maya," Alix announced. I glanced briefly away, at the other woman who'd yet to be given a celebrity, but it wasn't her who stepped forward.

Maya came straight toward me, holding her hand out and giving mine a gentle squeeze while the cameras moved and zoomed around us.

"Hi Alfie," her voice practically bounced with excitement. "I'm the assistant chef at a catering company, so I don't have as much experience as some of the other cooks here, but I'm hoping we'll make up for it with lots of energy!"

It sounded a little rehearsed, which it probably was, but the look on Maya's face was genuine enough.

And, well, I could do energy.

It was the cooking I was shit at.

Chapter Two
Maya

I've always loved cooking shows. Even before I knew how to julienne a carrot or poach an egg, I had an obsession with the Food Network. I would race home from school, wanting to spend as much time as possible watching those amazing celebrity chefs before my parents would come home and send me off to do my homework.

So when I saw a commercial that said a new show, *Serves You Right*, was specifically looking for chefs who worked in catering, I was obviously excited.

But I never meant to apply myself. I'd only been working with Catering by Daniel for six months. Since it was my first real job in the industry, it was more than stressful enough without adding a six-week competition on top of my regular working hours.

Even if I won the prize money, I didn't have the experience to set up my own company, no matter how cool it would be to pick my own events and get to create my own menu suggestions.

I sent the link to Sophie, my fellow assistant chef. She was three years older than me, and constantly complaining about how she wanted to be her own boss. *Serves You Right* could have been her chance to do exactly that.

When she said she was too shy to appear on camera, I didn't push her. Well, only enough to make sure she was really certain about what she might be missing. That was when she turned the tables on me. *If it's such a good idea, why don't you apply?*

And, well, I didn't really have a good reason.

Sophie helped me out, holding the camera while I talked about my love of cooking for big groups of people and why my favorite dishes to make are different from my favorite dishes to eat.

Once we'd sent it off, I did my best to forget about it, not wanting to get my hopes up. There was no way to know how many people would apply to be involved, but I was sure it would be a lot. They weren't going to pick me, not out of everyone.

But they did! I had to come in for an in-person audition, bringing along two dishes I'd made. Didi, one of the producers, said my chicken pot pie was the best she'd ever had.

After that, they had me sign a bunch of paperwork, including all kinds of insurance and liability waivers, and a 'code of conduct' which promised, among other things, that I wouldn't sabotage any of the other chefs or sleep with any of the contestants.

And then, just like that, they invited me to join them on the first day of real filming.

Before getting to the studio, I hadn't even thought about who my partner would be. I'd been more excited about the other chefs involved. And I definitely hadn't been wrong about that, because some of them were amazing!

Christine and Aaron were the head chefs of two of my absolute favorite restaurants - even if I could only afford to go to them for special occasions. And Renata had been working in Salt Lake City for long enough to be practically a legend.

Actors and musicians and hockey players just weren't as interesting. Not to me, anyway. I knew Sophie was a fan of Maxine's music, and mentally made a note to try to get her autograph later, in case either of us got kicked off in our first week.

Alfie, the guy they eventually paired me up with, was gorgeous, I'd give him that. If I hadn't known better, I would have assumed he was some hotshot actor, not a player for the local NHL team.

Knowing he played sport for a living *did* explain all the muscle in his shoulders, at least.

Trying my absolute best not to look starstruck, I gave him my rehearsed introduction, gripping his hand in mine to hold me steady. As one of the youngest in the competition, I knew I wanted to make a good impression on the audience. Maybe that would keep me in a bit longer, and give me more time to learn from this amazing experience.

Alfie didn't have time to say much in response - they'd already moved on to pairing up the last six contestants. Karl and Yuri were, like me, in the catering industry, though they had a lot more experience at it than I did. Karl was paired with Maxine, while Yuri ended up with the comedian, Hosta.

And that just left Garth, an actor, getting to cook with Seth, who'd written two cookbooks that I owned (and one I didn't yet).

It had taken a lot longer than I would have expected to get just a few minutes that could actually be broadcast, so Didi hurried us along to the start of our first challenge without any time for a break.

The rules were simple enough: Alfie and I each had to list three of our favorite ingredients. We had to pick at least one from each list to combine into a single dish that we'd serve to the judges, but we'd get bonus points if we included more.

It took me a long time to whittle my list of possibilities down to just a top three. I flushed as Alfie just stood there, having finished his list in about ten seconds flat. The challenge clock had already started, meaning that I was costing us valuable time.

Finally, I jotted down my last answer. A little breathless, I turned to Alfie. "Okay, that was way too hard! How did you manage to do it so fast?"

He gave a shrug, which didn't exactly answer my question. We were then told to set up for a 'reveal', where we'd turn our whiteboard to each other with the three items listed. I was kind of surprised to find that it felt a bit exciting. I was nervous, the competitive element completely new to me, but it was thrilling, too.

"I'm not like... good at food stuff," Alfie told me.

I wasn't actually sure what that meant. But then Alfie was told to turn around the whiteboard with the first of his items written down. It struck me how nice his handwriting was but that sense was quickly pushed aside as I frowned at what he'd actually written.

There it was, in beautiful curvy letters: *ketchup*.

"But... ketchup's not really an ingredient," I objected, the words flying out before I could think about whether it was a sensible thing to say.

Alfie's face didn't exactly fall, but he did look uncomfortable. Didi, meanwhile, ushered a camera to come in closer.

"Are you disappointed, Maya?" she asked, clearly enjoying the prospect that there might be some drama so early on.

"No, of course not," I said, shaking my head. I forced my lips to curve upwards. "Anyway, it's only one of three ingredients. I'm sure I'll be able to work with the other two."

I didn't want to dwell on my surprise at what Alfie had picked, but it was hard not to wonder why. I mean, ketchup was great, but there was no way I would ever have put it in my top ten ingredients, let alone my top three.

To move things along, I flipped over my own whiteboard. My top pick was zucchini. While it was super versatile, I wasn't sure there was a good way to include it and ketchup in the same dish...

"Yeah, I don't even know what that is," Alfie informed me.

I laughed, almost nervously, before it struck me that he wasn't joking. Alfie truly didn't seem to know. Zucchini maybe wasn't the most common of vegetables, at least that's what I told myself. I had no idea. I used zucchinis loads. But I'd give Alfie the benefit of doubt.

"Your next one, Alfie?" Didi urged and dread settled low in my stomach at her tone.

Alfie hesitated for a moment, like he wasn't quite sure he wanted to show me what his second board said. When he turned it around, I almost gave a sigh of relief. Just as prettily written sat the word 'cheese'. At least that was a real ingredient.

I grinned, nodding. Even though we'd only known each other a few minutes, I wanted to put Alfie at ease, to reassure him that his ingredients were fine. Cheese was something I could definitely work with, and that would go well with zucchini, which meant we were on much more promising ground already.

"I thought about putting cheese in my top three," I admitted, half to Alfie and half to the still-hovering camera. Actually, my choice would have been 'Gouda', specifically, but if Alfie didn't know what a zucchini was, it seemed like Dutch cheese might also be outside his field of experience.

My next option, which I flipped over at Didi's urging, was gnocchi. I'd wanted something comforting, which would also be a good vehicle for whatever other flavors ended up on our list.

Looking at Alfie's face, I regretted not just putting 'potato' down. It would've accomplished the same thing, but probably without intimidating a non-chef as much.

He stared at the word and then at Didi and then at the camera, despite having been told not to do that. Finally, his eyes returned to mine and almost apologetically, Alfie gave a small shrug.

"I have absolutely no idea what that is," he informed me, confirming exactly what I had expected. "Is that another vegetable?" he asked. Before I could reply one way or another, though, Alfie carried on. "I don't really eat those."

That completely distracted me from my mental debate over whether a potato-based pasta counted as being potato. "You don't eat... vegetables?" I repeated, stunned. Alfie shook his head. "At all?"

It was honestly hard for me to wrap my mind around. Of course, I knew some people were picky eaters. I'd been at school with some kids who wouldn't eat any vegetable except sweetcorn. But those had been kids.

Alfie was not only a fully-grown adult, he was also an athlete! I thought they were supposed to eat healthier than the rest of us.

"But ketchup's made of a vegetable," I pointed out.

"Smashed up vegetable," he shrugged. "I mean, I eat some vegetables. Like when they're in stuff. Like ketchup." That made no sense to me but I wasn't exactly sure how to express that either. Who didn't eat vegetables? Most of my meals were vegetables!

And, maybe more importantly, who didn't eat vegetables and entered a cooking competition?

My surprise must have shown, because Alfie gave me another apologetic look. "I don't think you'll be impressed with my third ingredient," he advised and well, now that I knew he didn't eat vegetables, it was highly likely that he was right.

Alfie turned his third board around, revealing something that I didn't think was even an ingredient, really.

Cereal, his board proclaimed.

Aware of the cameras, I forced myself to smile. Inside, though, I couldn't help but feel daunted by the sudden scope of the challenge I'd taken on. Cheese and ketchup and cereal weren't exactly the shopping list I would've wanted for myself.

"That might be a bit of a challenge," I admitted. My mind was whirring, generating as many ideas as I could come up with for unconventional ways to use cereal in a savory dish.

I'd seen people use crushed up cornflakes as a breadcrumb-replacement. But it was hard to see how I was going to combine that and any of my ingredients.

Alfie was hardly looking at me, and I felt a stab of sympathy for him. "Well, my third ingredient isn't a vegetable," I promised. "It's crab."

Truthfully, it wasn't exactly surprising when Alfie shook his head. "I've never had that either," he commented. In the grand scheme of things, plenty of people had never had crab before. But I did wonder if those who had, had ever had crab with ketchup.

"So now you have to decide what you will make with your... ingredients," Didi informed us, hardly masking her excitement at the idea of how much of a mess this could turn out to be. It was probably good for the show even if it wasn't good for us.

Determined, though, I gave a nod before turning to Alfie. He gave me another apologetic look. "I'm sorry. I knew this was going to be awful, my team signed me up for this."

Well, that explained that.

But I nudged Alfie in the ribs with my elbow, shaking my head. "Hey, now, you're assuming my creativity isn't up to the task. And you don't even know me yet." I tried to keep my tone light, to show that I was mostly joking.

The show had provided us with pantry ingredients, so I got started making some gnocchi while I tried to bolster Alfie's confidence in our ability. Maybe, by the time I'd done that, my creativity would've leaped into action.

"I want to make something that you can eat, too," I said. That wasn't part of the rules - I could have made something just for the judges, it would have been easier. But it also didn't feel very fair to exclude Alfie from eating something he was supposed to be helping me cook.

"Would you try crab?" I asked, curiously.

Only one camera stayed on us, with Didi off to get the other pairs to do their reveals. It felt a bit less like pressure and it was almost possible to imagine that the cameras weren't there at all. Not quite, but I could see how I maybe could get used to them.

"I mean, no," Alfie answered. "Like, I would never pick that. I'd try it... for this. Because it's rude not to." That kind of made sense, so I nodded. If he was willing to try it, that was a start.

Looking at the things I'd set out, Alfie frowned. "Will you tell me what to do? I know I didn't pick great ingredients, but I will try to help. There's a chance that I'll need pretty specific instructions," he warned me.

What we needed to do first was get the crab and the potatoes cooking, so I instructed Alfie to fill a pot of water and bring it to the boil, letting him drop the crab in while I continued to contemplate what our dish was going to actually be.

"I think I can work out how to use the ketchup," I said. "Gnocchi's like a kind of pasta, so we can do that with crab and make a sauce out of ketchup and something creamy." Maybe I could even use a mild cheese, that would be another of Alfie's ingredients.

"But I don't know about the cereal," I admitted. "Do you have any ideas?"

Alfie gave me a look that strongly implied he thought I was crazy for asking him. It was hard not to laugh at that. We were a team after all and even a broken clock showed the right time twice a day, right?

I told Alfie as much, making him snort. "Well, I once had some chicken that was coated in cornflakes, it was... kind of nice. Like fried? Can we fry a crab?"

And really, I didn't see why not. "We can try," I promised. "You grab some cornflakes and crush them up with a rolling pin or something. Maybe sure they're not the sugary kind."

Alfie gave me another look at that, but, after all, it was better to be safe than sorry.

"So, is there, like, a *reason* that you don't eat vegetables?" I asked.

He returned with a box of cornflakes and I watched him lay down a paper towel to gather all the crushed up cornflakes. For someone who didn't know to cook, that was actually pretty forward-thinking. Maybe this wouldn't be too much of a disaster. Still, we had to get through at least the first challenge.

"Dunno," he shrugged. "They just... don't taste good? Like to me. I know plenty of people love vegetables. Trust me, my nutritionist is all over that," he said, rolling his eyes. "But it's not my fault I think carrots are weird and mushrooms are gross. Is mushroom even a vegetable? Anyway, no reason. I haven't had some sort of a horrific encounter with a pumpkin or anything."

I couldn't hold back my laugh at that. It seemed to catch Alfie by surprise. For a moment, he tensed, then he glanced at me, saw me trying to stop, and a grin broke out across his face.

It made my heart do a quick tumble in my chest. "No, really, I'm glad you haven't had any horrible experiences," I assured him. "It was just funny." Somehow, the pumpkin had made it even more hysterical.

"Do you have to take a lot of vitamins?" I asked. "I mean, you've got a nutritionist, so -" I assumed someone was on top of all the nutrients Alfie might be missing from his diet.

"Some." He shrugged, beginning to roll the pin over the cornflakes more carefully than I had anticipated. "El, that's our nutritionist, she's pretty good at suggesting alternatives and coming up with meal plans," he explained.

As we went on, we fell into kind of a comfortable rhythm. Alfie was very good at following instructions and, actually, once we established what we were doing, we seemed to click together as a team. Both of us were a bit surprised by that.

"This... doesn't look awful?" Alfie commented as we dished up our fried, cornflake-covered crab meatballs, served with a creamy ketchup dip and a small gnocchi and zucchini bake with sprinkles of cheese on top of it.

"Oh, thank you," I teased. "What a lovely compliment that is." Alfie flushed, which made his handsome face look suddenly boyish and appealing. My tongue darted out, wetting my lips for a moment before I caught myself.

Just because my co-chef was a dazzling NHL star, that was no reason to drool over him where the cameras could catch me.

"I think it'll taste alright, too," I promised. "But I guess it's what the judges think that counts."

As it turned out, the judges loved it!

Both Alfie and I were a little surprised by just how much they seemed to enjoy what we'd done. They said that the cornflake coating made for an unexpectedly nice contrast with the softness of the crab meat. The sauce was the one thing that got some criticism, apparently tasting too sweet (which was the ketchup's fault, but hey, we'd tried).

All in all, we had done alright. While someone would be going away after this task, I couldn't help but feel a little hopeful about our chances. The decision as to who would leave wouldn't be announced until later, but Alfie and I were free for the rest of the day from filming.

Tomorrow, Didi informed us, we'd be expected to record our interviews and, after that, the results would be announced and we'd find out who'd be doing the challenge the following week and who would sadly be leaving.

Once the cameras turned off, Alfie gave the leftover food a look. "We should probably try it?" he asked, sounding almost a bit unsure.

"Yes!" In all honesty, I was more excited for Alfie to try it than the judges. Not only was he less likely to be critical, but I also wanted to show him that his suggestions hadn't been nearly as bad as he seemed to think.

Carefully, I rolled one of the deep-fried crab balls onto a plate, with a few pillows of gnocchi and some of the sauce. I wouldn't make Alfie try the zucchini if he didn't want to.

"Go on," I urged. "The judges wouldn't have said such nice things if it were awful."

I watched as Alfie bit into the crab ball, my stomach tying itself in knots. Crab was a pretty delicate flavor, but there were still plenty of people who didn't like it. If Alfie was one of them, I was just going to have to be okay with that.

His expression was impossible to read, which made my nerves even more prominent. I couldn't believe how much I cared about Alfie's reaction. When he finally gave a noise that sounded good, I grinned.

"It's... actually probably better than not awful," he decided, making me give a startled laugh. Maybe we'd work on Alfie's complementing skills. "Sorry! I mean, it's good. You did really well. I'm sorry for making it hard by picking ketchup as an ingredient."

"Don't be." I really didn't want Alfie to feel like he needed to keep apologizing. After all, he hadn't chosen to dislike the taste of vegetables, it wasn't something that he could help.

Even if I did hope that, maybe, we'd last long enough for me to find a way to serve vegetables that Alfie didn't hate.

"Look at it this way," I added, "I bet the judges were way more impressed with us for making something nice out of ketchup and cereal than they were with James and Aaron making something nice out of lobster and butter and garlic."

What I didn't say to Alfie was that Aaron's lobster tails had looked mouth-wateringly good. I was pretty sure they'd won the challenge, even if their task had been easier than ours.

Glancing at my watching, I groaned. "I should pack up - I've got a shift I need to get to. But I'll see you tomorrow, yeah?"

"Yeah." Alfie nodded. And then, after a moment's pause, his face lit up. "I'm glad I got paired with you, Maya," he informed me. "I'm sure the others are fine, but you seem pretty cool. I bet the others would have judged me much more outwardly for not eating vegetables," he teased.

I was about to object that I hadn't, but then, that would be at least partially a lie. So instead, I gave Alfie a small nod, my smile hopefully just as genuine as his was.

The day had been both more exciting and more tiring than I'd expected. The mix of the time-pressured challenge and having to constantly be aware of video cameras had left me buzzing, but I wasn't sure how long it would last.

As I packed up and drove to the venue we were catering at, I thought about what Alfie had said. Despite his limited list of ingredients, I was glad to have been paired with him, too.

The other celebrities might have been easier, but I doubted any of them would be as genuine as Alfie was in his willingness to help and be instructed.

Even though tomorrow was supposed to be my day off, I was looking forward to coming back for more filming.

But first, I had to help plate and serve fifty portions of perfect beef wellington.

Chapter Three

Alfie

It surprised me just how nervous I was about finding out the results of our challenge. Being competitive had always come naturally to me, so that part didn't surprise me. Usually, though, I was good at being pretty realistic, too. And I knew I couldn't cook. So if the challenge was a failure, then it wouldn't exactly be shocking.

Except we'd actually done alright if the judges' comments were to be believed. It was hard not to let that give me some hope.

That night, Chuck and Levi had come over, excited to hear all about how my first day of filming had gone. It had taken me about ten minutes of reading the contract I'd signed on my phone for me to figure out that I could tell them exactly nothing. I wasn't even allowed to tell them who I was paired up with.

Levi teased me for caring about some NDA for a reality TV show and normally I would have agreed. But the thing was, as I reread the contract, I realized that it wasn't just about me. If I was disqualified, Maya would be, too.

Somehow, in the few hours I'd spent involved with the show so far, I'd gone from not really caring to caring quite a lot. And that was all down to Maya. She seemed lovely. And even if I knew nothing about cooking, I could easily tell how much passion she had for it. Failing the show would suck, sure, but it'd be expected. Failing Maya would feel terrible.

I didn't exactly have high hopes for myself in the show, but I couldn't get us disqualified, that would be far worse.

So I diligently told Levi and Chuck nothing until they gave up asking. It wasn't without whining and calling me no fun, of course, but that was fine. The show would air on Saturday anyway so they could see who I was paired up with. I argued that it'd be more interesting that way. Levi didn't seem too convinced but at least Chuck let us move onto something far more important - video games.

The next day, I headed back over to the studio. The atmosphere felt a little calmer, maybe because most of us had overcome the first-day nerves. I chatted a bit with Maxine, asking about her experience yesterday. Apparently, the judges hadn't loved the salmon pastry dish that she and Karl had conjured. I felt a pang of sympathy for her but also some guilt for being pleased that Maya and I had perhaps done better.

When I spotted Maya arriving, I excused myself to go over to her. "So," I said before she'd even managed to get her jacket off. "Maxine says the judges didn't love their food, I think that's a good sign for us. Not for them, though I hope they make it through, Maxine seems super nice."

The look on Maya's face was purely sympathetic. "Oh, I hate that other people have to lose for us to win," she said, making me frown hard. I honestly didn't know what to say. Obviously, other people had to lose. That was just the way it was.

Maya chuckled, getting her jacket off. "I'm just... not very competitive, I guess," she admitted. It made me wonder why she'd entered a competition, if that was the case.

"It seems mean to hope that other people will be disappointed," she continued. "But on the other hand, I don't want to go out. And I don't want you to be disappointed."

"I'm not going to be disappointed if we lose," I waved my hand dismissively. "This matters to you more than to me, so I will be disappointed to disappoint you, but you don't have to worry about me."

It was true enough. The worst that losing would mean was that I would get endless chirping on the team about being shit at cooking. Since that happened anyway, it wasn't going to be very distressing.

"Maybe you just need to think about competition differently," I informed her. "Yes, you're right, someone will be disappointed, but it's important to use that disappointment to improve. Competition just means that you try a bit harder."

Slowly, Maya nodded. "I never thought of it that way," she admitted. I grinned, pleased that I'd been able to offer her a different perspective. And hopefully, one that would help.

"And," she added, "I guess everyone knew they were risking disappointment when they signed up. It's something that they've chosen as an acceptable possible consequence."

I nodded. That sounded pretty good to me. It was just like hockey, you didn't play unless you knew that losing would definitely happen sometimes.

"It would mean so much to me, if we did win," Maya said in a rush, her voice only loud enough for me to hear. "I know I'm young, but it would be great to be able to put it on my resume, even apart from the actual cash prize."

Her words made my stomach twist. Maya seemed really genuine and she'd been far nicer with me than my inability to cook probably deserved. If we didn't win, it would be because of me. But I would try. For her. She shouldn't lose just because I was shit.

"So far you seem really great, so hopefully that will sway the judges," I promised. "And you're very attractive, so I'm sure that has got to be considered by some producer somewhere, even if it doesn't improve cooking."

Most of the show was judged by the judges but - rereading my contract had reminded me - there were some audience voting components. Maybe Maya's looks shouldn't matter, but this was TV.

For a moment, Maya didn't say anything. She just looked at me. Unfortunately, I was never much good at telling what wordless looks were supposed to mean.

Was she annoyed that I'd commented on her looks? Or frustrated that they would matter when they weren't really anything to do with her career?

I couldn't tell.

"I think, when it comes to looks, the producers are probably thinking of you a lot more than they're thinking of me," she said slowly.

That made me snort, before I could even think about whether that was an appropriate reaction. "I don't think so," I shook my head. Like, sure, I looked fine, but Maya was genuinely stunning. The way her hair was pulled up in an unintentionally messy bun, the way her clothes fit just right, the way she smiled when she was pleased. And I'd only known her for one day and noticed all of those things.

"I mean, I suppose if it comes to it, I'll take my shirt off if it means we'll win, I promise." My promise was followed by a soft chuckle, but hey, I had had compliments before about my back and shoulders. Maybe if there was a challenge where you had to cook naked, I could overshadow my inability to cook.

But cooking naked did sound kind of unhygienic and I wasn't sure they could even show that on the TV.

This time, the widening of Maya's eyes was a lot easier for me to read. But as the surprise melted away, she gave me such a sexy smile that I felt my heart skip a beat.

"Well, at least if we ever get that desperate for points, there'll be an upside for me," she teased.

That sounded a lot like flirting, but Maya looked away almost as soon as she'd said it, making it hard to guess what I should say back. So I went with the obvious choice - saying nothing.

We headed over to our chairs, set in front of a background of various cooking implements. "I'm kind of nervous about this interview," Maya admitted. "I know I must have done okay in the tape I sent, or they wouldn't have picked me for the show, but that was just me and my friend Sophie messing around. This is a lot more scary."

Now, interviews were something I was genuinely pretty good at. Confidence soared within me at the thought that my ability to advise Maya on how to deal with this would be based on real experience.

"The trick is to just imagine that the interviewer is your friend Sophie," I told her. "Or well, any other friend. They ask questions that they know you can give good answers to. The hardest bit, really, is just to relax."

"Right," Maya muttered, but she didn't sound as if she agreed. "I'm not sure I'm very good at relaxing." At my puzzled look, she carried on. "I mean, I work pretty hard. People even say that I work too much. And I have a full-time job in catering, but here I am, entering a competition on top of that, so maybe they've got a point."

Working too much was something that Maya and I might have in common. Training with the Pumas was intense, and I definitely did my share of extra gym time on top of what our coach insisted was necessary.

But I also had the rest of the Pumas to help me switch off.

"Who helps you switch off?" I asked.

When she frowned, I went on. "Like who do you hang out with?" I realized then that maybe Maya had a boyfriend or a girlfriend, we hadn't exactly exchanged any sort of information other than me not eating vegetables and her working hard.

"Oh." Maya stammered a little, like my question had come completely out of the blue. It made me wonder, briefly, if she really was about to tell me she had a girlfriend.

She shrugged one shoulder slightly. "Well, Sophie at work. And I live with my cousin, Nadine. We're about the same age, but our schedules don't line up that much."

When I frowned, she explained. "Most catering events are in the evenings or at weekends," she pointed out. "Nadine works in an office, so she's usually home when I'm out, and vice versa."

"Gotcha." I nodded. "I don't think I know anyone who works at an office." Maybe one of the guys on the team had a girlfriend who worked at an office but I couldn't think of who. "Guess I'm lucky that all my friends do the same thing as me."

Which did mean I had almost no female friends; I always wondered if that was bad. I was pretty friendly with Chase's girlfriend, Morgan, but I wouldn't list her as a friend, not before Chase.

Maya smiled. "Yeah, that must be pretty cool," she agreed. "Do you get on with everyone? I've never really had a big group of friends like that. I can't quite imagine what it would like."

She looked up at me so sweetly that it made my heart hurt for her. If there had been a way for me to magic up a group of friends for Maya to have, I would have done it.

Sadly, the best I could do was tell her more about my experience.

"I'd like to think I get on with everyone," I said, shrugging. "I'm not equally close with everyone, but that's pretty fair in a team. They're still family, though." I smiled. It was true for most of us, thinking of each other as kind of brothers. But for me, it was probably even more true, since the team was the only family I had.

That was a bit too depressing to bring up when Maya and I had known each other for two days, if there was ever a good time. "So are you less nervous now?" I asked almost teasingly.

"No," Maya answered, but she gave me a grin as she said it. At least she was being honest, even if I would've preferred to have made her feel more at ease. "But you've distracted me nicely from my nerves," she added. "And I'll try to think of the interviewer as Sophie."

I wanted to reach out, squeeze Maya's hand with mine to give her a physical reminder that we were in this together. But we didn't know each other well enough.

Instead, I took the lead as much as I could during the beginning of the interview. It was easy for me. Talking about food and cooking wasn't as much fun as talking about hockey, but it was still basically the same.

What was more interesting, was listening to Maya answer the questions. For all her complaints about nerves, she didn't at all seem nervous when she answered the interviewer. Maybe imagining them as Sophie really had helped. But I suspected that it was more likely that it was food as a topic.

I was pretty experienced at listening to people talk about something they truly loved, but usually that was hockey. Hearing about Maya's love of catering, even if it was also in a discussion about her anxiety about the competition, was pretty cool.

"Thanks," Maya said, once we'd finished and they'd moved us on to take our positions for the hearing of the results. "You really helped a lot."

"Hardly," I shook my head. "You did so well!" And I honestly meant it. Of course, now we were getting ready for the results and nerves were starting to churn my stomach. I obviously wanted to not do badly, but that was just the competitive side of me.

Listening to Maya talk about her passions, though, made me want us not to do badly for her. "I really hope we don't get booted out," I hummed. "It'd suck to go out in week one, you deserve to stay longer and show them what you've got."

Maya beamed, looking genuinely pleased by my compliment. I hadn't even thought of it as being praise. It just seemed completely true that Maya shouldn't go out of the competition this early.

"I just hope they don't drag it out and make us wait forever," she said, laughing. "I always wonder if those long, unnatural pauses between words are edited in."

As it turned out, they weren't. Alix really did pause for so long after saying 'the winner is' that I could have counted to about a hundred.

It was James and Aaron who'd come first, impressing the judges with whatever technique they'd used to cook the lobster.

There was a small twinge of disappointment low in my stomach but it wasn't like I was surprised not to win. Before starting this competition, my expectations had been pretty low. Truthfully, maybe my expectations weren't all that high now, either. But it wasn't just about me any longer.

So, for Maya's sake, I hoped that we'd be one of the pairs who were safe.

As it turned out, we weren't even down to the worst two. They told us that it was in no particular order, but Maya and I were announced safe next. It felt a bit surreal, both of us looking at each other to check that we'd heard it right.

The competition had already moved on. It was between Maxine and Karl and the YouTuber Legacy (who, I had to admit, I had Googled the night before) and Renata. It was kind of tough because they were both great pairings, but I couldn't help but lowkey hope it'd be Maxine who got to stay. After chatting a few times, she felt more like a friend than Legacy or Renata.

My nerves about Maya getting kicked out too soon had eased. But it still took forever and a day for Alix to finally reveal that it was Legacy and Renata who wouldn't be coming back next time.

They seemed to take it pretty well. Renata came around and hugged each and every one of us, wishing us the best of luck and promising that she'd be watching the show to see how we got on.

Maya looked both relieved and saddened. "Renata was so lovely," she said softly, once the filming was over. "I suppose that's the worst of a competition like this, somebody has to get eliminated."

"Yeah, but that somebody wasn't us," I pointed out. There was a voice at the back of my head that whispered 'this week', but I was pretty successful at ignoring it. What mattered was that we hadn't gone out first. Somehow. It felt pretty unbelievable when considering that I literally couldn't cook.

But Maya definitely deserved to be here, so I would do my best to just follow whatever she told me to do. How hard could that be, right?

"Alright guys, that's a wrap for the first week!" Didi announced. "We're having a little after party, though admittedly it's mostly nibbles and wine, but please do stay and get to know each other better."

That was probably both a blessing and a curse. Working with these people, it'd be good to know them better, but if we became friends, it'd be all the more difficult to wait during these eliminations.

"We should probably mingle," I decided.

The truth was that I actually would have preferred to stick around Maya. I'd only known her for a day and there was very little I actually knew about her, yet... I kind of wanted to learn more. Still, it wasn't a good look to just stick together.

And frankly, I didn't want there to be any rumors that we might break our contracts or something.

We were in this together. But that didn't mean I should find Maya attractive.

It just felt a bit more of a challenge than the cooking.

Chapter Four

Maya

At the party, Alfie led by example. Even though we separated, my gaze kept darting back to him, taking in the breadth of his shoulders and the surprisingly light way he moved. He chatted to everyone. Not just his fellow celebrities and my fellow chefs, he also talked to Alix, the host, and Jay, one of the cameramen.

I was too far away to hear what he was saying, but it all looked effortless. It made me feel a little jealous. I'd never been that easy with people, and the idea of actually approaching any of the celebrities made my palms itch with anxiety.

Still, Alfie was right, we should make an effort. So, after chatting to Renata, who was definitely the least intimidating person in the room, I forced myself to go over to Maxine.

She must have been able to tell I was nervous, but she was super nice about it. She even gave me her autograph when I asked, and offered to bring in a copy of her autobiography.

By the time I got home, I was physically exhausted, but far too emotionally keyed-up to sleep.

Luckily for me, my cousin, Nadine, was actually home for once.

"Guess what I have?" I singsonged, waving the photograph Maxine had signed. "I brought you back a gift from my fancy celebrity party!"

"Oh my God! Is that from Maxine Deveraux?" Nadine asked, snatching the autograph from my hands. "I didn't even know that's who you're up against," she commented and that made me realize that, oh yeah, she wasn't meant to know. The first episode was out the day after tomorrow and until then we weren't to tell anyone anything.

It was a bit embarrassing how easily I'd failed my NDA. Nadine knew me well, though, practically reading my mind. "Don't worry, I will accept this as a bribe," she promised. "Are you going to tell me more about how it's been going, though? I haven't seen you since you started yesterday. Did you do the first challenge already? You must have if it's airing in two days."

Suddenly, I was very aware of all the things I wasn't supposed to tell Nadine. Everything was barred, from what the challenge had been to how it had gone and even who I'd been partnered with.

But I couldn't just say *nothing*. "Yeah, we wrapped up the filming," I answered carefully. That was probably okay. After all, Nadine and I lived together. She was going to know when I was out and it wasn't for work.

And, somewhat pathetically, I was rarely out for non-work and non-filming-related reasons.

"It's really exciting," I admitted. "I mean, mostly being around all those other chefs. Competing against them, trying to come up with the best possible dishes because I know I'll be compared to them."

"Leave it to you to be more excited about the chefs than the celebrities," Nadine laughed.

It was true, though my mind did also instantly jump to Alfie. Maybe he wasn't exciting in the same way as the other chefs were, but it was hard to deny that something inside me perked up when I thought about him.

Nadine, having known me since I was a child, gave a loud 'ooh' at the expression that must have crossed my face. "It's like that, is it?" she exclaimed. "Come on, you've got to tell me. I promise I won't say anything to anyone. It's only two days! But I will die if I don't find out," she informed me seriously, making me snort.

She did make a good point. Nadine, along with the rest of the world, was going to find everything out in two days anyway. What harm could it do if I gave her a little preview?

"Okay," I said, making myself comfortable on the sofa, "but I'm not going to tell you who won, or who got eliminated. You'll have to watch the show for that."

There was plenty I could tell Nadine without breaking those self-imposed rules. And I knew just what she would be the most thrilled by.

"I got paired with an NHL player."

"Oh my God!!" she exclaimed so loudly that it actually startled me. I laughed; it was kind of the reaction I had been hoping for. Nadine was a huge fan of hockey. She'd tried to take me to games, but I just couldn't see past the sheer aggression of the players to find anything beautiful about the game itself.

Being paired up with Alfie, though, definitely made me a little bit more interested. Or well... it made me interested in him.

"Is he like super hot?" Nadine asked, clearly needing to establish the important details there.

There was really no choice but to admit that Alfie was. "Yeah," I said, making my eyes go wide as I nodded. "Sometimes, I get distracted just looking at him." It had happened at least twice at tonight's party.

"And you don't even *like* hockey," Nadine exclaimed. And she was right, for me to see past the fact that Alfie played in the NHL meant there was really something special about him.

But that wasn't what I wanted to talk about. "But he doesn't eat vegetables, Nadine. How can anyone not eat vegetables at his age?"

"He... what?" She blinked and yes, that was exactly the sort of reaction I'd expected. When Alfie had told me, it had been surprising. I wondered if they'd show that on the TV. Probably. There would be other people, especially people watching a cooking show, who would be as shocked as I had been and as Nadine was.

"No vegetables? How does... how does one play a professional sport and not eat vegetables? Is he allergic or something? Can you be allergic to all vegetables?" I was pretty sure that a lot of people were allergic to raw vegetables, but I also knew that wasn't Alfie's problem.

"He just... doesn't like them," I answered. And, honestly, that didn't make any more sense to me than an allergy. Because vegetables tasted so different. I could understand not liking zucchini, for example, or not liking fennel or squash or tomatoes. But how could you dislike all of those things, when they didn't even taste the same?

Part of me wanted to cook Alfie one of my favorite vegetable dishes, something that he'd have to like. But I also didn't want to push. I imagined that he got enough of that in his life without me adding to it.

"I mean, I don't have to cook things he can eat, necessarily, but I kind of want to, you know? If he's going to be involved in cooking it with me, I should make an effort to make things he'll want to eat."

Nadine seemed less convinced of that argument. "I think you should focus on winning the competition," she argued. "Is he at least... helpful? I suppose the whole point of the competition is that the celebrities are a bit of a hindrance? Unless they can cook. Are there some who can?"

I wrinkled my nose. "There are some who certainly think they can." James had spent a good twenty minutes telling me all about his 'amazing' barbecue set-up and how he liked to make his chicken wings so spicy that none of his friends could even handle them.

To me, that just sounded like James was being an inconsiderate host. Of course, I hadn't told him so.

"Alfie claims not to be able to cook at all, but he's done well at following my instructions." It was nice, feeling like Alfie trusted me, even when I'd suggested three ingredients he wasn't familiar with.

Nadine gave a mock sigh of relief. "That's good, then," she nodded. "It'd really suck if you were paired up with someone who was a dick. Especially someone who was hot and a dick," she joked with a grin.

That was probably true, my mind instantly jumping to how much I wouldn't want to have been paired up with James. The others seemed nicer, but the arrogance that James oozed didn't seem very good for teamwork. Then again, Aaron didn't seem to mind. And they had won the first challenge.

"So what did you have to do? Was it fun? Were you nervous?" Nadine barraged. "Sorry, sorry, I just want to know everything. I'm very impatient."

"I was so nervous!" I answered first. "I still am, a bit. I mean, about it being on TV and people - strangers - watching!" While I was confident in my ability to cook, I was very aware that the audience wouldn't actually be able to taste my dishes. It was weird, thinking that they'd be judging me based only on how I described them and what the judges said afterward.

But the fact that Alfie was so very positive and open definitely helped. "I'm sure the viewing public will adore Alfie," I told Nadine. "That's who I'm paired up with. He was so apologetic about not giving me better ingredients to work with, and not knowing how to cook."

And his being gorgeous wasn't going to hurt, either. Remembering that Alfie had said people might take *my* looks into account, too, I blushed.

"But it was fun, too," I added. "It was way more of a challenge than I expected it to be. I don't get the chance to actually come up with my own menus very often." At least, not for an audience larger than Nadine and I. She let me cook whatever and she did all the washing up into the bargain.

"I can't wait to see the first episode," Nadine sighed. "It's only two days, I know, but it feels like forever. Especially now I know I have an attractive NHL player to look forward to," she added with a laugh.

The fact that I was going to be on the TV was still something that hadn't quite sunk in. But once the first episode aired, things would become more real, I was sure. And we hadn't gone out in the first week. Of course, there was no knowing what the next challenge might be.

But whatever it was, I'd have Alfie at my side. He'd come up with a surprisingly good idea of using the cereal to coat the crab balls, so whatever our second challenge was, hopefully we'd serve something just as good.

"I had to sign a contract saying I won't have an 'intimate relationship' with anyone on the show," I admitted to Nadine, flushing only a little bit. "But I don't think I'd want to flirt with someone while we were both being filmed." Flirting was bad enough when I was only running the risk of embarrassing myself in front of one person, let alone however many people tuned in to watch *Serves You Right*.

Even though I knew they existed, I could never go on one of those reality shows where dating was the whole point. "Alfie did tell me that I was pretty," I added, teeth catching against my lower lip as the memory warmed me from the inside. Luckily, he'd said it while no cameras were running.

Nadine laughed at that, shaking her head. "Well, you are pretty," she teased. "And while I get where you're coming from, I think a bit of flirting on camera might be a good thing. It'll make for good TV."

The face I pulled even at the idea must have been funny, because there was another deep laugh that rumbled up from Nadine's chest. It was pleasing to make her laugh, but I definitely had no intention of flirting on TV for entertainment value. It was, of course, pretty difficult to know whether just being me would appeal to the audience, but I had to trust that the producers had picked me for a reason.

"So did Alfie tell you that you were pretty because he was flirting with you? Was this on camera? Do I get to see your reaction?"

Gratefully, I shook my head. "No, this was before an interview. Nobody gets to see my reaction to the hot NHL star telling me how very attractive he thinks I am." Which was good, because the look I'd given Alfie had been half-stunned and half trying to work out whether he was kidding.

While I didn't think I was ugly, I'd also never considered myself to be particularly attractive. I was just... average. At college, before I dropped out to switch to a career in catering, I'd experimented with different styles, and even dyed my hair different colors, trying to make myself more striking.

But it was all a lot of upkeep, and in the end, I'd fallen back into the habit of keeping my hair its natural color, wearing it in a bun that was usually messy by lunchtime, and wearing shoes that wouldn't hurt my feet if I was standing for hours.

"I don't think he was flirting," I said, realizing I hadn't given Nadine an answer. "But I don't know why he'd point out my being attractive when there are actual celebrities like Maxine Deveraux around." Maxine was gorgeous. Any man would be far more likely to give her a second look than me.

The look Nadine gave me heavily implied that she thought what I'd said was dumb. Still, she was a good enough person not to tell me that. "I'm sure he said it because he meant it," she informed me with a confidence Nadine couldn't possibly have since she hadn't met Alfie.

But if she had met Alfie, Nadine would probably say the same.

Nothing about Alfie had seemed fake or like he'd tell me something like that without meaning it. "But obviously you've signed this contract. What happens if you break it? Do you just get thrown off the show?"

"That's what the contract said," I confirmed. "That they could impose 'disciplinary action' up to disqualifying us from the competition." And for me, getting kicked off the show was the last thing I would want!

This was my chance to really make a name for myself in the industry, in a way that years of just showing up to work and never making a mistake couldn't replicate.

It wasn't that I wanted a shortcut, exactly, because I still wanted to earn whatever reputation I left *Serves You Right* with. It would just be a much quicker, much riskier way of earning it, which appealed to something in me.

"So, that's two reasons not to flirt with Alfie, no matter how cute he might be."

A tiny voice in my head whispered that both those reasons were definitely temporary. There was nothing to say I couldn't flirt with Alfie after the competition was over.

But I wasn't enough of a fool to expect that he'd have time for me once he no longer had to see me for filming. Even from the little he'd told me so far, his life sounded pretty busy. Besides, he might have a girlfriend already.

"There's nothing to stop you from flirting with him, though, if you meet him through me." Even saying the words, I was hit with a sudden wave of jealousy. It was ridiculous, but I didn't want Nadine to flirt with Alfie.

Worse still, I didn't want Alfie to flirt with her…

"Um, no thanks," Nadine rolled her eyes. "Like, I'm sure he's great, but it feels a bit weird." Relief swept through me at her words. Not that I had any claim to Alfie! Especially not when I'd signed an actual contract that forbade me from any 'intimacy'.

Nadine shook her head. "It's going to be an interesting few weeks," she decided. "So you're seeing everyone next week for filming again? What until then? Just... work?"

The way Nadine said it made me wrinkle my nose. She was a good friend, as well as a good cousin, and she always tried to get me to have more of a social life.

But in truth, I had nothing planned except for work and more work. And reading cookbooks, which nobody but me believed was a hobby.

"I might watch a film or something," I said, a little defensively. I'd been wondering whether I could find something that James had been in. Maybe he'd be a little less off-putting if I'd seen him play someone nice on screen.

Seeing as Nadine was actually home, for once, I added, "You're welcome to join me. I'll even let you pick something from my Netflix list."

"Such generosity!" she exclaimed, shaking her head. Her tone, though, gave away her amusement and I grinned back. "Alright, alright, we can do that. But you'll have to cook. Nothing difficult, I don't want to exhaust you for your competition. Just keep you on your toes, be ready, be prepared."

I rolled my eyes at that, but I was rarely against cooking. Nadine was always a very appreciative audience. And at least she liked vegetables.

It was a relief to be able to experiment with whatever ingredients we had in the kitchen, knowing that nobody was going to be judging the results.

But my mind did keep straying to Alfie, how I could adapt what I was making into something he'd be willing to try.

Strangely, instead of my distraction leading to disaster, it seemed to push me into making one of my best experimental meals ever! At least, Nadine said it was the most delicious thing she'd ever eaten. I didn't tell her that I'd been thinking of preparing it for someone other than just the two of us.

Chapter Five

Alfie

The day of the first episode airing came around in a blink of an eye. For a moment, I had wondered if I should ask Maya whether she wanted to watch it together. That seemed kind of weird, though, and I figured that she must have friends or family she wanted to watch it with instead.

Besides, a bunch of guys had invited themselves round to my place for the premier already.

We were all crammed into my living room, to an endless amount of complaints about how I should have gotten a bigger house. They weren't actually wrong. My house was... normal. It wasn't a huge luxurious palace like most of the guys on my team had chosen.

The honest truth was that when I'd bought it, I hadn't really been thinking about how big or expensive I could go. Growing up without any spare money ever, I supposed I was pretty frugal. Usually, though, the reminder of that only came when six hockey players tried to squeeze into my living room.

"Shhhh!" Chuck shushed everyone dramatically. "It's about to start!"

Everyone did shush then, but it didn't last long, the room erupting in wolf whistles when my smiling face appeared in the credits, 'Alfie Reeves' in glitter gold.

"Our very own superstar," Chase teased, waggling his eyebrows at me. It was ridiculous; I definitely wasn't the most famous member of the Pumas. The only reason none of the others had ever been on reality TV was that they'd chosen not to.

Maybe next year, I'd get them back by entering them on one of those dancing shows.

But for now, I smiled as Maya appeared on the screen, bobbing as if she were listening to music while she whisked something in a big bowl. It definitely wasn't something that had happened while I'd been with her, so they must have filmed the chefs' intros separately.

I almost pointed her out, then remembered that the whole point of the first episode was to show us pairing up. The guys would just have to wait.

Still, Felix did start with 'so who did you get?' before being smacked up the back of his head by Levi. "We're going to find out," he informed everyone very seriously. It was kind of funny just how seriously Levi was taking this, but also pretty sweet. In fact, having the guys here to watch the first episode with me was very nice of them.

"Right, fine," Felix muttered, but did turn back to the TV. The introductions were mixed in with the announcing of the pairings, so James and Aaron got their little intros once their pairings were announced.

It wasn't long before my intro flashed up. Watching myself on the TV felt weird. I'd obviously seen myself give interviews before, but mostly I just watched tape of hockey, like everyone else. This felt very different.

"Here we go," I nodded when it was finally time to say who'd I'd been matched up with.

"Oooh," Chase cried when Alix read out Maya's name. "You got the pretty one!"

As far as I was concerned, Maya didn't look half as good on the screen as she did in person. But I had to admit, she did still look pretty good. I was sure that Maya being so attractive was going to mean we were popular with the audience, just like I'd told her.

Of course, she'd said that the audience would find *me* attractive, but I was definitely not going to tell the guys that.

"So is she nice?" Levi asked. "We know who you got paired with now, so you can tell us whether you got on well, right?"

"Ah, yes, Levi's in with the important questions," Chuck snorted. "Is she *nice*?" he repeated, mockingly. The thing was, Maya was actually very nice and I was pretty happy to be allowed to say that now that they knew who I was paired up with.

Ignoring Chuck, I gave a nod. "She is. We got on pretty well. I hope it shows on the show." And of course, once everyone else was paired together, they cut to the challenges and a strategically placed commercial break, starting just after a clip of me telling Maya I didn't eat vegetables.

It made the guys burst out laughing.

"I hope they don't send you home this week, Alfie, this show is already my favorite and we haven't even seen the cooking," Trevor announced, throwing some popcorn at me and making me roll my eyes.

"Poor girl," Levi added. "She looked... thunderstruck." That made me squirm uncomfortably. Maya had taken my substandard ingredients pretty well, but it still made me flush to think about the fact I was putting her in a much harder position than any of the other chefs.

When the commercials were finished, after a short clip of Aaron and James agreeing on everything, the show cut to Maya asking me *why* I didn't eat vegetables.

She looked sympathetic, at least. That was more than I could hope for from the rest of the Pumas.

"Aww, I hoped she was going to make you eat a real vegetable," Chase said, pouting. "She's a chef, she shouldn't be enabling you."

"I bet the black-haired one would've done," Levi commented.

"Yuri," I said. I'd taken extra care to learn everyone's name. Yuri was paired with Hosta who was a comedian. She was... well, I could see why Levi would think she'd force me to eat vegetables. Yuri was very much a no-bullshit kind of person, but the show seemed to amp that up a lot more, too.

The challenge really started then, the cameras showing all of us preparing our ingredients. There weren't actually a lot of shots of me and Maya, the camera mostly focusing on the people who were struggling more.

It made me feel a little proud about how Maya and I had done. By the time the next commercial break rolled around, the guys started arguing about who they thought should go home.

"James looks like a dick," Levi announced, making me snort.

"Yeah, sure," Chuck nodded. "But he's not going to be going home. Not with how he and Aaron are making that lobster."

"Oh, are you now a chef, Chuck? Shall we sign you up for the next series?" I snorted.

"I'd do better than you," came the predictable reply. "At least I wouldn't choose cereal as one of my favorite ingredients!"

And, really, it was hard to argue with that. Cereal was great, and I genuinely did like eating it, but I knew that it wasn't what Maya would have expected. After all, she'd had to ask me if I had any ideas on how to use it.

"I think Legacy ought to go," Trevor announced. "He seems to be letting Renata do all the work. It's not very collaborative."

"Oh, so you think I'm doing great?" I teased and Trevor snorted.

Levi, being the friend he was, reached over to pat my back. "You're doing a lot less shit than we all expected," he informed me in a tone that made me smile. There was something very brotherly about it. Of course, then he had to go ruin it by adding. "I bet that you are going out in week three, so if you can do that, that'd be awesome."

"Wait, you guys bet on when I'll leave the show?" I frowned.

It shouldn't have surprised me. And, after a few moments of indignation, I decided that I didn't really mind. The only part of it that irritated me was that betting on me leaving was also a wager that Maya would leave. And Maya deserved better than that.

"Don't worry," Chase said, tossing his beer can into the trash as he spoke, "nobody bet on you to win, so you don't have to worry you're disappointing anyone."

"You're all assholes," I announced. Then, after a moment's pause, I frowned. "Wait, can *I* bet on me winning? I feel like someone should." And while it didn't at all surprise me that no one had, I felt like it was a little mean.

Then again, I literally couldn't cook, so fair.

Chuck shrugged. "I don't see why not?" he asked, looking around at the other guys who all nodded. "It's fifty dollars to enter," he informed me. I could spare $50 to bet on myself.

"...since no one else will," I muttered, handing the money over.

As if sensing my annoyance, Levi shrugged one shoulder towards the TV. Maya was plating up, asking me to hand her things while she focused on keeping the plate clean and the food exactly the way she wanted it. "That doesn't look half bad," he said. "I'd eat it."

The rest of the guys chorused their agreement, and it did take a little bit of the sting out of their lack of faith in me. If they had to think I was going to lose, then at least I could surprise them along the way by producing actually decent food.

"Did you get to taste it?" Chuck asked.

"Did you even want to taste it?" Chase added. "I've never seen you eat crab."

'Want' was probably pushing it a bit. The idea of trying crab hadn't exactly appealed to me, but Maya had asked me so nicely and I was quickly finding myself struggling to say no to her.

"I did try it," I answered. "It was... surprisingly nice, actually. The reason you've never seen me eat crab is that I never had. The cornflake coating was good." And while it had definitely been good because Maya had known how to make it, I did feel a little proud of myself for having suggested it.

The episode went on and the kind of nervousness we'd felt at the elimination came across well. I was surprised to see how many of the contestants seemed to fidget, something that I hadn't noticed at the time. Maya was one of them, though, I had known she'd been nervous.

"Oh come on, how long do they drag this out?" Levi sighed dramatically. "Was it like this on the day?"

"Yeah," I nodded. "Just even more tense, because I know who gets voted out," I added with a small chuckle.

Nobody was particularly surprised when James and Aaron were announced as the winners. Their dish had looked professional, and the judges had praised them a lot for whatever technique Aaron had used.

When Maya and I were the next to be announced as safe, the guys cheered, patting my back. Even Chase, who'd bet on me to go out in the first week, told me that I'd done well.

It was surprisingly enjoyable, hearing them all applauding my efforts. I kind of wished I had invited Maya after all, in case whoever she was watching with wasn't as demonstrative.

"Look, look," Levi interrupted, pointing at the TV. "I was right, they are sending that Youtuber home."

"Aw, that sucks, I liked Renata, she reminded me of my gran," Chuck whined.

It made me think of my nana and how much she would have loved this show. She would have liked Maya, I was sure. Nana always had a soft spot for nice girls. And who could blame her, really?

There wasn't a trailer for next week, which was understandable since we hadn't filmed yet, so the show finished instead with an interview with Renata and Legacy. They both talked about what a great experience it had been, which seemed a bit much.

"We literally filmed for two days, a few hours each day. Mostly, it was just stressful." Though, they probably weren't allowed to say that.

Chase tutted. "Don't be soft, Alfie. How stressful can it really be helping a pretty girl to cook something that you gave her the ingredients for!"

But despite the chirping, it really had been. Not so stressful that I really minded, of course, but enough that I worried about letting Maya down.

In a way, the two of us were a team, just like the Pumas were a team. The main difference was that I knew I was actually good at hockey. Cooking was still something I didn't think I'd do well.

"You're good at being on a team, though," Levi pointed out when I voiced some of that concern. The other guys nodded too, which helped. It made me smile a little. For all their chirping and betting for me to go out in the first episode, I knew they had my back.

"And you're less of a dick than James," Chuck added, making everyone laugh.

"I'm so much less of a dick than James that unlike James, I've got some more beers for you assholes," I announced getting up to a chorus of cheers.

After that, it was beer and video games with a side of pizza. I could almost relax enough to forget to worry about what next week's cooking challenge would be. It was probably telling that I felt more anxious about that than the game we had between now and then.

~*~

When I agreed to go on *Serves You Right*, our coach had been pretty clear. I was only allowed to do the show if it didn't affect my gameplay. So far, nothing seemed to have changed, but there was still a sense that it was important to push myself harder. I hadn't gone out in Week One, so it was time to prove that I could do both things.

Tonight was the perfect opportunity. We were playing the Boise Bluebirds and everyone was in good spirits. Luke's speech before the game had been, in my opinion, one of his best. It always made me think about how good Luke was at this sort of thing, I wondered if he got some sort of captain training for pep talks.

It felt like even the ice was on our side as we skated out to the cheers of the home crowd. Home games were always the best games. They did come with extra pressure, of course, since no one wanted to let down a whole audience full of fans.

Still, the chanting and encouragement gave everyone a huge buzz.

We seemed to hone it as the game started, the first line doing well. Felix and Chase did some great passes between them, before sending the puck towards Flynn. It bounced off the goal with a sharp ping that got muted by the shouts of the fans.

Close but not quite.

From then, the game got more aggressive. The Bluebirds went on the offense, their puck pursuit so aggressive that it made us regroup. Olle managed to protect the goal the first time the Bluebirds' center shot it towards him, but the relentless attack ended when one of their wingers scored an empty net.

It was not a great place for us to be, but a line change later, we were back on track. A pass from Levi hit the shaft of my stick, letting me flick it just at the right angle for the goal. It felt a bit miraculous as the sounds went off to tell me my attempt had been successful.

The first period saw us skate off with an equal score and, if anything, it seemed to lead Luke to give us an even better pep talk.

As it turned out, it was all for nothing, because the Bluebirds scored within the first few minutes of us returning to the game. Whatever the pep talk their captain had given, it was clearly a good one.

With a pass shooting across the ice, my eyes were peeled for the puck. It shot towards the goalie, but bounced off just at the wrong moment. Still, Luke and Will seemed to go at it with newfound aggression, both of them chasing relentlessly until Will's assist led to another goal.

It left the third period as the deciding one. We all pushed hard, skating faster and more precisely. Adrenaline cruised through me as I led the puck across the ice, my ears pounding from the noise of the fans and my desire to score.

My pass never reached its intended target, though, sliding just past Levi's stick. Thankfully, the noise around us drowned out the loud curse I let loose.

The pass that Chuck shot back went much better. It hit my stick easily and I turned it over, skating just fast enough to send the puck flying towards the Bluebirds' goal.

Score!

With a goal's lead, all we had to do was make sure they didn't retaliate. Playing harder and faster, I felt the sweat drip down my body. We had only a few minutes left before the game was finally over.

My body ached as we moved off the ice, but the sense of victory made it all worth it. Despite the fact that tomorrow was filming, I agreed to go out with the guys to celebrate. Just one drink, I'd promised myself.

So when I got home at three in the morning, my body was absolutely exhausted, and there were six different alarms set on my phone.

Chapter Six

Maya

The first week of filming had been both exciting and nerve-wracking. Everything about it had been new, even the actual cooking, since I'd had to improvise with Alfie's ingredients.

The second week felt a little closer to normality. After watching myself on screen for the first episode, I was still very, very aware of the cameras as we were all lined up where the producers wanted us to stand. The show's hairdressers had brought my hair down again, framing it around my face in a way that would never be allowed in a professional kitchen.

"Really, we should all be wearing hairnets," I muttered, prompting a titter of laughter from the other chef contestants. I did understand that it wouldn't look as good on TV. It would certainly be a shame to hide any of Alfie's handsome face under a hairnet or a hat.

Speaking of Alfie, he was very quiet at my side. Last week, he'd been constantly in motion, but today he seemed content to let everyone else talk, allowing the words to wash over him. Nothing particularly caught his interest, which made me wonder if he was distracted by something going on in his life.

"Are you okay?" I asked, quietly enough that no one else could hear.

Almost with a start, Alfie lifted his head, offering me a small, sunny smile. "Yeah, I'm fine. Just tired. We had a long game last night."

That I could understand. I'd already had to go straight from filming to a shift at work. I could hardly imagine how much more draining it would be the other way around.

"So, what did you think of the show?" I asked, assuming that Alfie had watched it. "Is it the kind of thing you'd usually sit down to see?"

"No," he answered instantly. The answer itself didn't surprise me, but it did startle me how sharply the feeling of disappointment hit me. I loved cooking shows, it was what had made me want to go into cooking, at least partially. Alfie's answer felt a little dismissive of that, even if all he had said was 'no'. Maybe it was the speed at which he had said it.

But I did my best not to show that reaction, because I did recognize it as a little silly. There was no reason why Alfie would be into cooking shows, especially as someone who not only didn't eat vegetables but admitted to that on TV.

"I'm guessing you do?" he asked, oblivious to the turmoil going on inside of me.

I smiled. At least Alfie wasn't dismissing cooking shows for everyone. "I love them," I admitted. "I mean, I grew up watching them. I think I learned more from watching cooking on TV than I did from my parents."

It made me a little sad, that there weren't any family recipes that had been passed down to me, or that I would be able to pass on in turn. Neither of my parents really cared about cooking.

"Not so much the competitive ones," I admitted. "Though I find those more interesting now that I know enough to actually guess how certain flavors will go together, or how hard certain techniques are to master."

"Well, you certainly know more than me." It was hard to tell from Alfie's subdued tone whether he was teasing, or if it was simply a statement of fact. "Honestly, I don't think I've ever even watched a whole episode of a cooking show. Like the food looks alright, but a lot of it also just looks weird? It's never like... easy recipes. I had to Google how to boil eggs."

That startled a laugh from me and Alfie shrugged unapologetically. There was something very charming about the way he wasn't embarrassed about his lack of cooking skills.

"Oh, no, I am embarrassed," he promised me when I pointed out how it didn't seem like it. "But I'm also really used to people mocking me for it. The whole reason I got signed up to this show was that the guys thought it'd be funny."

Oh. Somehow, that made me feel a little sad, as if it somehow proved that Alfie didn't think much of what I did for a living. But I really had no reason to believe that. He'd been nothing but supportive of me last week, and seemed to really want us to do well because of the good that would come of it for me.

"I don't think it's something you should be mocked for," I said honestly. "Obviously, they're your friends, but it sounds a little mean."

Maybe I only thought so because I loved to cook so much. But none of my friends would mock me for anything that I couldn't do.

"I don't think you need to be embarrassed, either. I'm not embarrassed that I don't know how to play hockey."

"Oh, no, it's not mean. Like, sure, I do get that it sounds mean, but it's just... Teasing - chirping - it's a big part of playing hockey. Team building, I guess. The guys don't do it to make me feel bad."

It wasn't necessarily something I could relate to, but I nodded anyway, taking Alfie's word for it, since I had no experience with it. "And I think playing hockey is a bit different. You don't need to play hockey to survive."

There he paused, giving me a small grin. "Well, *I* do, but most people don't. But you do need to eat to survive, so it's pretty important to know how to cook. I can cook some things but... simple shit, you know?"

I nodded. "Of course. I had to start with simple stuff, too." Maybe I'd started younger than Alfie had. My interest in cooking had developed far earlier than most people I'd been at school with. That was the only difference, though. Well, that and that I actually liked far more ingredients than Alfie seemed to.

"You obviously know how to cook enough to survive," I pointed out. After all, Alfie had made it to this age, and he'd already achieved a lot in terms of his career. "Why should you be embarrassed that you can't do more than that?"

I didn't really expect Alfie to answer. Embarrassment wasn't rational, but I'd still wanted to tell him my perspective. Maybe it would make him feel a little better.

"It'd be different if you wanted to learn," I added. "But... I assume you're happy with how you eat now?"

The question seemed to make him pause, like he hadn't actually considered if he was happy with the level at which he knew how to cook. "I think I eat fine," he finally decided. "But other people don't, not really. I'm not malnutritioned or anything, but El's always on my back about trying more different things."

El, from what I remembered, was the nutritionist that Alfie had mentioned, so it wasn't too surprising that she'd be encouraging him to eat more varied things. "I suppose I'm just a fussy eater," he shrugged. "Growing up, my nana just made the things I liked."

It made me smile. Making food that someone you loved liked was, at least in my experience, the greatest sign of how much you cared about them.

But I was also curious. If Alfie's nan had done most of the cooking for him, I wondered where his parents had been. It hardly seemed appropriate for me to ask.

Especially not as Alix had stepped up to give us our instructions for the challenge. We were to prepare as many canapés as we could in an hour of cooking. There was no limit to the ingredients we could use, but we were encouraged to keep them looking as consistent as possible.

"Alright, I think we can do this if we work together," I told Alfie. "We can come up with a routine and try to do each one the same way as much as possible."

The way Alfie nodded and seemed to listen intently was a good sign. It seemed like the sort of challenge that would definitely benefit from his willingness to work with me. Despite the tiredness that was still noticeable, Alfie focused on the task at hand.

Or well, so I thought before he leaned in a bit closer, whispering to me. "I don't know what a canapé is." Despite his best efforts to keep quiet, from the way the camera snapped to us, I knew his microphone had picked it up just fine.

I made an effort not to sigh. After all, there was no reason that Alfie should know. Unlike me, he hadn't worked at a hundred cocktail parties. In fact, I doubted Alfie had even been to half that many. I might not know much about the NHL, but they didn't seem like cocktail party people.

"It's just a small bite to eat, like the kind of thing people send round at a wedding while the photographer is getting all the official photographs. Enough that people aren't drinking on an empty stomach, but not so much it'll spoil their appetite for dinner."

Even if he didn't go to cocktail parties, maybe Alfie had been to a wedding or a gala or something where they'd have served that kind of food.

"If we want to avoid vegetables, we could do cheese puffs. And while those are in the oven, we can put together some spicy chicken skewers."

They hadn't said we had to produce multiple types of canapé, so I was hoping that doing two might impress the judges, especially since we could do so easily.

Or so I hoped, anyway!

"Okay." Alfie nodded. "Cheese puffs and chicken skewers," he repeated. "Just tell me what you want me to do and I'll try my best." It was such an easily offered promise that I found it hard not to smile at Alfie.

He hadn't lied either. Once we started things, all I had to do was give Alfie instructions. He didn't question what I did or how I did it. My mind jumped back to what Nadine had asked, about whether the celebrities were a hindrance.

In some ways, there was a part of me that felt Alfie should have been one. He didn't cook, he didn't even eat most of the things I cooked, he didn't know food names, for God's sake. Yet, it was difficult not to appreciate how helpful he was.

Every so often, he'd look up to give me this small smile, like he was pleased to just be helpful. It made my heart beat so hard in my chest I worried that the microphone might pick it up.

We were working in such a companionable silence that when an argument started from James and Aaron's table, it was impossible to miss it.

"No, no, no," Aaron shouted. "Not like that. They have to be consistent!" I glanced up, trying to peer across the room so I could work out what Aaron and James were making.

Everyone else was doing the same, of course, so I couldn't get a good enough look to be certain, but it looked like they were wrapping something in strips of bacon.

"They look fine!" James insisted. Even from a distance, I could feel him roll his eyes. "If we spend all our time fussing about them being exactly the same size, we'll only be able to make half as many as everyone else."

Alfie glanced over, too, before looking back at our canapés and then at me. "Are ours looking good enough?" he asked. "I mean, they look the same to me, but I assume there's like a... chef's point of view? Do you train in recognizing if food looks the same?" The way he grinned at me told me that his question was a joke.

It struck me that, unlike James and Aaron, Alfie and I actually worked together well. I'd never truly been in charge of instructing someone else, only stepping in where my head chef needed me to, but this didn't feel hard.

Aaron and James continued to argue, voices getting louder and louder. I'd seen some pretty aggressive head chefs in my time, but it still made me flinch. Alfie, however, barely seemed to notice.

I suppose, compared to a crowd of NHL fans, James and Aaron probably didn't seem that loud to him.

"I think they look consistent," I answered. "They're not identical, but I think there's a balance of getting the appearance to be good enough and still producing enough food."

Since I worked in catering, and not in a restaurant, this challenge played to my strengths.

"Cool, cool." Alfie nodded with a soft hum. The cameras had moved away from us to focus on James and Aaron. It made me wonder if that was a bad thing for us. But I didn't think I was someone who could arrange things in order to get more camera time. Looking at Alfie, I wasn't sure he was either.

But before I could ask, he gave a loud hurrah at having managed to roll one of the cheese puffs perfectly on his first attempt. The sheer joy on his face made my stomach flip and a wide, genuine smile appear on my face.

"Are you proud?" he asked, head snapping to me, his smile lighting up his whole being, it seemed.

I'd thought my heart was beating hard before, but it must have tripled at the idea that Alfie wanted me to be proud of him. That my opinion would matter to him at all made me grin from ear to ear.

"Yeah, I'm so proud," I confirmed. "You're doing amazingly, Alfie. For someone who claims not to be able to cook, you're making so much progress!"

And the cheese puffs ought to be something Alfie would actually like eating, too.

The praise seemed to somehow make him smile even wider. "You make it pretty easy," he informed me. It contrasted a lot to the way Aaron and James were still arguing. I looked away so my blush wouldn't be too obvious. Alfie, though, didn't seem to notice.

"Is this something you do at work, then? Making many tiny foods?" Alfie asked as he moved on to fill another tray full of the little cheese puffs.

Watching Alfie work, I couldn't help but notice how strong his hands were, how carefully he was shaping each puff before setting it down just as I'd shown him. Heat flamed into my cheeks as I wondered how it would feel to have Alfie touch me with so much care and attention.

Once I'd allowed the thought into my head, it was as if something had cracked, a flood of similar images filling my senses.

It was only when Alfie called my name that I realized I was supposed to be answering a question!

"Yeah," I said, grateful that Alfie couldn't read my thoughts. "We do a lot of parties and weddings, so lots of tiny foods." My smile widened, my body relaxing as I thought about cooking. "I always wanted to cook for lots of people."

"Really?" he asked, sounding genuinely surprised. When I frowned at the question, Alfie shook his head. "It's literally not something that has ever occurred to me as something to want," he explained. "I mean, sure, cooking isn't for me, I'm pretty sure, but even so, what's... what do you find so appealing about cooking for lots of people?"

The interest that shone in Alfie's eyes made me feel almost giddy. It wasn't something I had a lot of experience with, someone being genuinely interested not only in what I did but why I did it.

Perhaps that was why my trembling hand twisted one of the cheese puffs entirely out of shape.

I discarded it, using the moment to cool myself off. "I suppose it's the atmosphere," I answered. "Food is such a big aspect of community, we see that all through history. No matter where you go in the world, or what time period, people celebrate with food."

It was something I'd read a lot about, but I didn't want to gush too much. After all, it was really only interesting to me. "Weddings, graduations, promotions, anniversaries, they're all occasions to get people together to eat. I like feeling as though I'm part of the good times in people's lives."

I couldn't read the look Alfie gave me, but he didn't exactly offer me the opportunity to try for long, looking away. It felt a bit like he was forcing himself to focus on the pastries but maybe that was just me projecting what I hoped he thought. And even so, why would he even think that about me, right?

"That's not a way I've ever thought about it," he commented. "It sounds... nice. Being involved like that. Kind of like having a big family? Maybe? I don't really know, I didn't have a big family growing up. Did you?"

I filed that away, adding it to what I already knew about Alfie's upbringing, which wasn't much. But it felt weird to ask him such personal questions when I knew there were cameras hovering around us.

It also meant I didn't want to be too open about my own answer. I doubted whining about my childhood was going to make me popular with people watching.

"Not really," I replied, keeping my voice light. "I'm an only child, so it was just the three of us at home. I have cousins, but we only got to see them once a year or so."

That wasn't too revealing, and I could easily change the subject. "It's stressful, too," I admitted. "Working on big events, knowing how important they are! I'm actually going straight from this to a bat mitzvah. A once-in-a-lifetime event like that, you really don't want there to be any mistakes."

"Oh," Alfie said, frowning. "Is that normal? For you to be stressed about work? Or is the show making it harder?" It was a very fair and genuine question, but Alfie must have seen how my eyes snapped up to the cameras.

He gave a small shrug, moving in a little closer to me. I was sure it was meant to be comforting, but all it did was make my body heat up with pure *want*. Oh, God, this really was not going well for me.

"Is there anything I can help with? With your work? I'm really good at folding cheese puffs," he joked.

It made me laugh, easing some of the tension I'd been carrying. "You're really sweet, Alfie."

As soon as I said it, I wished I could call it back. It was true, but Alfie was so much more than sweet! Besides, I really didn't want my feelings splashed all over the TV.

"Didn't you say you were exhausted from your game? My shift's probably going to go pretty late."

It was generous of Alfie to offer, but I really couldn't take him up on it.

"Sure, but you aren't going to ask me to play another game of hockey, are you?" he pointed out and I shrugged, like I wasn't quite sure. Not that I could keep that up for long, before bursting into giggles. Alfie grinned, too.

"No, but really," he commented then. "If you think I can help, I would be happy to, just let me know." There was such genuineness in his tone that I truly didn't doubt that Alfie meant it.

Before we could talk more about what Alfie could or couldn't do to help, the first of my oven timers beeped, letting us know that the first round of cheese puffs were ready to plate.

After that, everything happened in a rush. We finished the chicken skewers, Alfie making sure they were all in neat, straight lines while I put together a quick dipping sauce.

When all our canapés were spread out across our table, even I was impressed with how many we had. Considering Alfie wasn't a professional caterer, we'd worked together exceptionally well.

Garth and Seth hadn't been so fortunate. The judges said that the canapés they had managed to produce were delicious, but they'd only put together a dozen mini quiches, nowhere near as many as any of the other teams.

It was a shame, but nobody was particularly surprised when Alix announced that Garth and Seth wouldn't be joining us for the third challenge.

Seth was nice about it, joking that he'd make use of all the recipe ideas we'd given him in his next book.

We bid them a regretful goodbye, then they let us leave. Alfie once again offered to come with me, if he could be of any help. I did my best to turn him down politely - after all, a complete novice in the kitchen would probably be more of a liability than a help.

But I carried the warmth of his offering with me all night. Sophie noticed me smiling to myself, and I was glad we were too busy for her to grill me about who was making me look like a love-struck fool.

She'd make me spill the beans eventually, but I was safe for today, at least.

Chapter Seven

Alfie

Like with the first episode, the guys crowded into my living room to watch the second one. There was less teasing about my inability to cook, though only just. While Levi had laughed that I hadn't known what a canapé was, I felt a bit better when some of the other guys admitted they also wouldn't have known.

Having witnessed the argument between James and Aaron, I wasn't surprised to see it covered pretty extensively on the show. It was high drama, after all. The guys rolled their eyes. Chuck even went as far as throwing some popcorn at the screen.

What I hadn't expected was how much the cameras had caught the way Maya and I worked together. They showed glances that I was sure hadn't even been there. It had to be editing, the way Maya looked away from me, a soft smile playing on her lips.

Except there were also glances from me.

"Oh, oh! Is romance in the air?" Trevor asked in a singsong voice.

And that was kind of it. Now, instead of being teased about not being able to cook, I was getting teased about my crush on Maya. I couldn't even really deny it, because while there definitely was some editing magic... well, I wasn't going to admit to the guys that it was true.

The rules had been clear, so I mostly just worried that the way they were portraying Maya and me, someone would say we were breaking them. But some well-edited looks couldn't do that, could they?

It had to be editing. I would have noticed if Maya had looked at me like that.

The guys didn't seem to care for that argument, instead deciding what mine and Maya's 'couple name' would be (Alfaya) and then heading to social media to see if other people thought so, too.

As it turned out, within hours of the second episode airing, #alfaya was trending on Twitter. Someone even sent me a picture of mine and Maya's heads Photoshopped onto the couple from some romance film I vaguely remembered watching years ago.

It was... weird.

When we turned up for shooting the next episode, it was days later. By now, there were even articles about how 'cute' we were. I worried about how Maya was reacting. While rumors about who I was dating weren't something I encountered often, I was fairly used to the media's eye.

Maya? Not so much.

So when we met up - at a farmer's market of all places - to film that day, I gave Maya a small bump with my shoulder against hers. The cameras weren't rolling yet, so I didn't have to worry about how it might come across.

"How you doing, the better half of #alfaya?" I asked a little teasingly.

Instantly, Maya's face went scarlet. It made me feel bad that I'd brought it up without some kind of warning. My intention hadn't been to embarrass Maya, and yet that was clearly exactly what I'd managed to do.

"It's so silly," Maya managed to squeak. "I mean, there's two other male-female pairs. I don't know why the editors have picked on us."

She couldn't quite look me in the eyes as she continued. "I hope I haven't done anything to make it easier for them to film us that way," she said softly. "But if there's something you want me to stop, well, I'll try."

The meaning of what she said took a moment to sink in. Then, I shook my head. "No, no, don't be silly," I reassured. It hadn't even occurred to me to worry about it. Mostly, my worries had been focused on Maya and how she'd be taking this.

"I'm not usually popular enough for the press to be making shit up about me, but it's hardly the first time," I promised Maya. "I... are you okay? It's a lot of publicity that I'm sure you're not used to."

It wasn't until a few days ago that it had occurred to me how different Maya's experience of this must be. Sure, I mostly got filmed in games and interviews, but there was still a publicity element to that. Maya... cooked food.

"Oh. Um." Maya's teeth sank into her lower lip in a way that almost looked painful. I had to consciously resist the urge to reach out with my thumb to encourage her to ease the pressure.

She shrugged one shoulder. "Well, I had to stop reading Twitter. There were a few people questioning whether I was 'good enough' for someone like you." She made the quotation marks with her fingers, looking resigned to the whole thing.

"It's not that big a deal," she assured me. "I use Instagram way more than Twitter, anyway."

There was no good way to respond to that; it made me instantly angry. Who were these people out there, knowing what would or what wouldn't be good enough for me? In the time I had known Maya, there was no doubt in me that there was no one she wouldn't be good enough for.

But I couldn't say that.

So it took me a moment to figure out what I could say.

"No one makes better deep-fried crab balls than you, so those people have no idea what they're talking about," I informed Maya confidently. I was, in fact, confident of both of those things.

When she smiled, I latched onto it, smiling back. "Come on, do you know what we're doing today? Shopping, I guess?"

Maya nodded. "Well, pretend shopping," she informed me. "We don't actually need to buy anything for the next challenge. Didi hinted that there was going to be some kind of competition over who gets to pick their ingredients first."

Pretend shopping sounded, if anything, more boring than regular shopping.

"We just walk around, look at some ingredients, they might ask me some questions about what I like to cook with or how I pick things out."

"That sounds…" I managed to stop myself in time before actually saying that I thought it boring. Maya had clearly described it as something exciting. Grocery shopping, to me, had never been fun and frankly, I wasn't really sure how it could be for anyone.

Maybe it felt to Maya like how shopping for hockey gear felt to me.

"I mean, I'm glad you'll be having fun," I finished, realizing I hadn't actually concluded my sentence.

Maya laughed, just in time for the cameraperson to tell us that they were rolling and we should start our pretend-shopping excursion.

Probably because she knew I didn't like vegetables, Maya didn't stop at the first farmer's stall, instead making a beeline for one that had a whole tub full of apples.

"How do you feel about fruit?" she asked me. "I know it's probably got more sugar in than you're allowed to have a lot of, but what about as an occasional treat?"

"I'm allowed to eat apples," I laughed. Whether I *wanted* to eat apples was a different question. Unlike vegetables, fruit I found a bit easier. Probably because it didn't need to be cooked. Well, I supposed maybe we would cook it if Maya chose to get apples.

This didn't feel much like a challenge, just us browsing different foods. But then, I supposed it wasn't meant to be a challenge. It was just Maya and me, which did make me wonder if there'd be more footage edited to make us look... well.

The thought made me take a step back, but only slightly. "I'm even partial to a clementine," I informed her, my tone light and teasing.

For a moment, Maya's smile made me think she would tease me back, but she just nodded, her expression pleased but still serious. "Clementine's are good," she agreed, "sweeter than oranges. And smaller."

She moved around the stall, until she found the citrus fruits. There were only oranges and lemons, no clementines, and Maya pouted.

I wanted to move on, to at least see what other stalls the farmer's market might have to offer us. Maybe there would even be something other than food, though I knew I was unlikely to find hockey gear.

"How do you feel about cherries?" Maya asked.

For a moment, I wasn't sure if Maya's question was a trick one. Cherries, surely, weren't fruit. But I felt a bit dumb for saying that in case I was wrong. Even I knew that tomatoes were fruit (though, El had tried to use that as a way to convince me to eat them). But berries...

"Cherries are fine," I decided. "And strawberries, blueberries. I don't like the weird ones, though." Maya's eyebrow rose at that, obviously not knowing what the weird berries were. "Gooseberries. The orange ones? They're very round and kind of hard but also squishy. They're gross."

"Cape gooseberries," Maya answered. I had no idea whether that was the right answer, but it was very impressive nonetheless. Collecting a paper bag in one hand, Maya selected several of the things I'd said I liked.

Before I could point out that she'd said we didn't need to buy anything, she answered my unspoken objection. "I feel bad standing here, making them think they're going to sell something, and then just walking away."

Glancing up at the stall-holder, I frowned. It honestly wasn't something I'd considered, but I could kind of see how Maya might feel bad about just browsing without buying anything.

. "I'll pay for it with my own money," she added. "The producers are hardly going to mind as long as I'm not using up any of their resources."

"No, I'll pay," I rushed in to correct, reaching out to stop Maya from reaching for her wallet. Our hands brushed against each other, electricity sparking between us. I pulled my hand back, but almost definitely not before a camera had already caught it.

Turning away, I handed some cash over to the man behind the stall. When my eyes returned to Maya, her focus was on anywhere but me.

"Sorry," I said quietly, glad that we weren't miked up for this. I looked over at the cameras and then back at Maya. "I feel bad that the press is making such a thing about us, like bad that it's happening to you because of me." And I certainly wasn't helping by accidentally touching her.

Maya shook her head, still not meeting my eyes. "I don't think it's because of you," she said. "I mean, you haven't done anything to make it look like you want to date me, or anything."

A mixture of relief and disappointment swept through me. While I was glad that Maya didn't think I was breaking our *Serves You Right* contract, it also saddened me that she would think I *didn't* want to date her.

Though, if her idea of fun was a farmer's market, I wasn't even sure what kind of date we could go on that we'd both enjoy.

Keeping her distance, Maya carefully took the bag of fruit, waving a hand towards yet another stall of food. "Come on, we can let them film us trying different kinds of cheese," she suggested. "And then, once I know what you like, maybe I can put it in our next recipe."

I wrinkled my nose, but I supposed I had agreed to this, even if I hadn't imagined I'd be spending my time with a pretty girl sampling different kinds of cheese.

~*~

Unlike the filming of stock footage of us walking around a farmer's market, the actual challenge that day was a lot more fun. I was confident that we would ace it, too. It was a string of athletic challenges. Running, jumping, balancing.

When they had announced it, a thrill had shot through me.

I might not be able to cook, but I could do athletic challenges!

We'd work together to gain, steal and trade ingredients that we would then end up cooking with. It involved little strategy, just figuring out what we wanted. But when I asked Maya what we wanted to work towards, she'd looked at me like I was crazy.

At first, I wondered if she was just doubting my ability to achieve whatever goal we set. It seemed to motivate me even more, like I wanted to prove myself to her. Rather than focusing on what that was about, all of my energy went into these challenges.

I obviously volunteered to start us off, especially since the first challenge involved running and lifting bags of flour. Between Maya and me, I was stronger. It made sense for me to do this. Tex, the reality TV star, turned out to be pretty strong competition.

By the time I moved the third huge bag of flour across the room, I was covered in the stuff. White clouds surrounded me as I dropped the bag to rush and get another. My heart was pounding but I knew how to do this. Adrenaline powered through me, the competitive nature kicking in hard.

When the challenge finished, there was flour sticking to my wet forehead. But we had also won!

"I mean, he *is* an actual athlete," James complained. "Are we going to get an acting challenge?"

"So I could win that, too?" I chirped back, so used to that being the appropriate sort of response to give. As *three* different cameras snapped towards me and my flour-covered face, I realized it probably was not appropriate in this scenario.

It was hard to feel too bad about it, though, when Maya was trying to hide her giggles behind an upraised hand. And James looked positively thunderstruck, which just made the rush feel all the sweeter.

"You did really well, Alfie," Maya praised, keeping her voice down a little. I could still hear the gratitude and the admiration in her tone, though, which made my heart swell against my ribs.

Maya had been so instrumental in our success so far, it was great to think I'd actually be making life easier for her by winning us whatever ingredients she wanted.

The cameras were still circling and Maya glanced toward them before holding up a dish towel. "Here, you should probably rub some of the flour off."

"Oh, thanks," I laughed, taking the towel from her. I wiped my brow first, the flour dusting off me in some places, but I could almost feel it congealing with sweat. "Ugh, this is gross," I whined.

Turning to Maya, I pulled the towel away from my face. "Is there more left?" I asked since we had no mirrors nearby. The crew were setting up the next task now, something that seemed to involve a jump rope. Since it was me who did the first challenge, there was a great chance Maya would have to be doing the next one.

"Yes," Maya answered, deadpan. I groaned. Maya gave a furtive glance towards the cameras, which they definitely caught, because they were all pointed at us and away from the crew.

Part of me knew that Maya shouldn't help me clean up. It would definitely just add fuel to the fire of the gossip surrounding #alfaya.

But even so, my heart skipped a beat when she reached for the dish towel, carefully brushing it along my jawline.

Our eyes met and I could almost hear the way Maya breathed in. There was absolutely no doubt in my mind that this was going to end up being aired on the show. Yet, it was hard to pull back, to brush it off. Maya looked so good, standing close enough that the light smell of her perfume practically surrounded me.

"Thanks," I murmured when she'd wiped the flour off, her hands dropping. She didn't immediately take a step back.

For a moment, it felt like time stopped, like both of us were waiting for something. Whatever it was, the moment seemed to break when Maxine loudly wondered if the jump ropes were going to be hard.

I could practically see Maya's face pale, especially given how close she still was. "I hope I don't undo all your hard work," she said softly.

At first, I assumed she was just being self-deprecating, but the longer I looked at her, the more I realized that Maya was genuinely nervous.

"If I'd known there was a chance I'd have to do something athletic on television for anybody to watch, I wouldn't have put my name forward," she muttered. "I suppose it must say in one of the contracts that we have to participate in every challenge."

"You'll be fine," I promised, but truthfully, it was not a promise based in fact. In the few weeks we'd known each other, we hadn't had to do anything physically challenging. Not more so than balancing some trays or cutting stuff up. Maya was definitely awesome at those.

But maybe she wasn't awesome at jumping rope.

"Whatever happens, it's fine," I decided. "You'll just have to blow them away with your cooking and I know for sure you can do that."

Maya's cheeks went pink, but she looked more pleased than embarrassed, so I figured I must have done well in my attempt to encourage her.

And I hadn't even had to say anything that wasn't true. If Maya could cook well enough to keep us out of last place with cheese and cereal and ketchup, there was no way she was going to lose us the competition with whatever ingredients we ended up with today.

"I'll do my best," Maya promised, "but you don't give yourself enough credit. It was you who came up with the idea of using the cornflakes to deep fry the crab balls."

She grinned. "So, as long as you're still on my team coming up with ideas, I'm sure we'll be fine."

That made me smile back widely. "I'm always on your team!" I informed her happily. I genuinely enjoyed being Maya's teammate, too. It felt like we were on an actual team. Looking out for each other, supporting each other. I'd only ever had those sort of experiences with the Pumas.

This was new.

But I liked it.

Chapter Eight

Maya

Alfie's words had made me feel better, but nothing could completely remove the horror of taking on an athletic challenge on television.

It wasn't that I was unfit. My job kept me on my feet for such long hours that I burned off the calories in what I ate almost without noticing. And since I was always conscious of my budget, I'd walk anywhere that I could, rather than spend money on gas.

If the challenge had just been running, I could probably have handled it.

But I'd always been badly co-ordinated. In gym class, I'd struggled on the balance beam, or with throwing the ball in the direction that I'd meant. It had even taken me hours of practice not to nick my fingers with the knife when I was dicing vegetables.

Any challenge involving a jump rope was just about my worst nightmare.

I was sure Alfie thought I was exaggerating. His expression totally gave it away. It was sweet, really. Alfie seemed to think I could do anything in the world, just because I'd managed to whip up something edible from his ingredients.

Once they waved me forward, though, Alfie couldn't help but begin to see the problem. The challenge was relatively simple: if I jumped rope ten times in a row without tripping, I could claim one ingredient. Then, if I did it twenty times, I could claim another two, and so on until we ran out of time.

My sweating palms gripped the plastic handles and I really tried to focus on bouncing up just in time for the rope to swish under my feet.

One.

Maxine was next to me, but I couldn't allow her to distract my attention. The rope came down again, whistling past the floor and under my sneakers.

Two.

But the next time, I must have brought the rope over too early, or lifted my feet too late. I stumbled, momentum coming to a halt.

I didn't dare look at Alfie, though I was aware of him beside me. What was a professional athlete going to think of someone who couldn't even jump rope? School children were better at this than I was, and my cheeks flamed with burning heat.

"Come on, Maya! You've got this!" he told me first quietly, but when I did look up, Alfie nodded energetically. "You did two! Now you just need to do... another two and then two more. You've got this!"

I really did not have this.

Yet, there was something so ridiculously sweet in having Alfie cheer me on. Unfortunately, it didn't seem to make me any less clumsy. This time, it was the fourth jump that made me trip.

It was hard to imagine that my face could get any redder. This would be seen by so many people! It felt like embarrassment was exploding through me.

"Hey, hey," Alfie said, drawing my attention to him. "Just go slower," he told me. "Focus on me, come on, I'll jump with you," he informed me and then jumped as if to demonstrate how he'd do it with me.

It made my heart lurch. I'd expected Alfie to be frustrated at my incompetence but if he was, he was hiding it extremely well. And I wanted to win us at least *some* ingredients. That way, we wouldn't lose all the advantage that Alfie had earned us.

So I tried to do as he said, slowing down so that the rope didn't tangle around my ankles.

I got all the way up to six, but then, feeling a flush of relief, I made the mistake of glancing away. The sight of Maxine next to me, jumping so fast that the rope was an actual blur, toppled me off balance immediately.

"I can't do it," I whined, my chin tucked against my chest so I wouldn't have to meet anyone's eyes.

"Of course you can," Alfie told me confidently.

What struck me was that he was paying absolutely no attention to the cameras. All of Alfie's focus was on me. It made me blush, but almost luckily, the way my face was already completely red from the embarrassment and jumping masked it pretty well.

Somehow, the sheer belief Alfie seemed to convey did actually work. I jumped again, and just like he'd done the previous time, Alfie jumped with me. When I managed ten, he gave an honest-to-God cheer.

It was ridiculous, part of me knew that. But more of me felt a surge of triumph. I'd done it! Ten jumps might not seem like a lot to anybody else, but for me, it was an achievement of the highest order.

Even so, I didn't know if I could do *twenty* jumps in a row. I turned, about to ask Alfie whether I should risk it, but I hardly needed to. His belief in me shone out of his face, making me feel weak at the knees.

I took a step towards him, sure that if I closed the distance between us, Alfie would wrap his arms around me and lift me up.

Then I caught myself. Alfie had made it clear when we were shopping together that he wanted to downplay those rumors about us. Me jumping into his arms was going to give exactly the wrong impression.

"I'll try again," I said, forcing myself to turn back to face the camera. "Maybe I can get us another ingredient."

The smile that Alfie shot me seemed to light his whole face up and, despite how terrible I felt about this whole exercise, it was impossible not to smile back at least a little. Of course, once I started jumping, the clumsiness made itself felt once again.

I did a good job of not swearing, but it was a close call.

"Look, you're doing great!" Alfie cheered me on and I gave him a skeptical look. "You've done a lot more jumps than you thought you could," he argued.

He definitely had a point. I hadn't thought I would be able to do ten, and I had, so maybe doing twenty wasn't completely out of the realms of possibility.

I forced myself to try again, keeping my pace steady and letting Alfie count for me as he jumped along with me.

Watching Alfie seemed to make it a lot easier to judge when the right time was to jump. I just waited until he exaggeratedly bent his knees, then I bounced up into the air as the rope swished under my feet.

As the rhythm of it carried me along, I made it to ten, and then to fifteen, and then I tripped once more.

But instead of feeling crushed and stupid, elation raced through me.

"Fifteen, Alfie! I made it to fifteen."

"You did!" he exclaimed with equal amounts of excitement. It felt so strangely validating. I could almost forget about why we were doing this. Almost. But this time when I started again, it was easier. I focused on Alfie, focused on his jumps and his encouragement.

I jumped my twentieth jump just as Alix called time. "Twenty," Alfie announced, sounding so excited. "You jumped twenty times and didn't trip, check you out, Maya," he informed me, genuinely sounding proud.

A week ago, I would have thought such praise was excessive. I might even have said it sounded patronizing. But Alfie wasn't just saying it, he seemed to genuinely mean it. He understood that, for me, I had really achieved something that I'd believed was impossible.

If that was how all Alfie's team-mates were with one another, I could almost understand the bond he talked about.

"I couldn't have done it without you," I admitted shyly. "You kept me going when I wanted to give up."

"Well, that's because we're a team," he informed me, almost echoing what I had been thinking. It felt pretty great to be on a team with Alfie. It made me want to always be on Alfie's team. I didn't know what I was meant to do with that particular thought.

Thankfully, I was saved from trying to say something about it by Alfie carrying on. "You should come see me play tomorrow night," he said. "We've got a game, so you should come. Bring a friend, whatever. I've seen you work, it only seems fair."

I winced. In all the time Alfie and I had known each other, I hadn't exactly told him that I just didn't like hockey. Not that I'd ever tried playing it, but Nadine was a fan and she urged me to watch a few games with her.

It wasn't something I'd enjoyed. Or even something I could imagine myself enjoying.

But, as Alfie had said, it was only fair of me to come cheer him on.

So, doing my best to hide my reluctance, I agreed. Alfie promised to put tickets aside for me, which meant there was absolutely no way I was going to get out of it.

It was only one night, though. I could watch one night of hockey, if it was for Alfie.

Naturally, Nadine was delighted that she'd lucked into free tickets to watch the Pumas play. Even if she did have to 'babysit' me for the duration.

"It's going to be fine," she insisted. "Honestly, it's just a game. You can watch baseball, I don't know why you have such a problem with hockey."

As far as I was concerned, baseball was a very different thing, but I knew that it would be no use trying to explain that to Nadine. She loved hockey and found baseball too boring for words.

"It's just so... overwhelming," I tried to explain. Even waiting in line to collect our tickets felt like an assault on my senses. There were people everywhere, shouting and laughing, a sea of fans in their team's colors. "And then the players move so fast, I can't keep up." In baseball, it was easy to keep my eye on the ball and feel confident that I would see everything important. Whenever Nadine and I had watched matches on TV, I'd lost sight of the hockey puck within minutes.

I didn't want to bring Nadine down, though, so I let her lead us to our seats. Anxiety and excitement swirled together in the pit of my stomach. It was impossible not to feel a little claustrophobic in the crowd, but this was a chance to see Alfie outside of filming.

Nadine talked me through a few hockey terms, hoping it would help me keep up with the commentators. The more she explained, the more I felt as though my head was swimming. There was no way I was going to be able to take all of this in.

"I'll just do my best to watch Alfie," I decided. That was why I was here, after all. "You can tell me anything important that happens." Nadine laughed, but she accepted that it was the best offer she was going to get out of me for the night.

When the players started streaming onto the ice, my eyes eagerly searched for Alfie's familiar face. It was hard to tell the guys apart when they were all wearing helmets, but I finally spotted 'REEVES' across the back of a jersey and eagerly pointed it out. "There he is!" I practically squealed.

I'd never thought Alfie looked out of place in the kitchen, but it was obvious that the ice was his natural habitat. He moved so fast and so smoothly, swooping across the crisp surface of the ice and keeping his stick low to the ground.

Suddenly, I felt my mouth go dry. I'd always known Alfie was attractive, but seeing him like this was something else. He looked powerful, his head down as his skates drove him forward, shouldering his way between the other players. It made me so much more aware of all those muscles that I'd admired before. This was *why* Alfie looked the way he did. Seeing it in person made me feel like my insides had turned to boiling liquid.

Once the game actually started, it was hard to keep track. I did my best, leaning forward and shifting from side to side as the players moved across the ice, but one blue-jerseyed Puma looked much like another.

Nadine didn't have to tell me when something important happened. The whole crowd reacted to every shot on goal, the noise almost deafening as it came at me from every angle.

Even knowing Alfie was there, I hated it. It was just too much, and the guy on my other side seemed to get more animated by the minute. He was practically shoving me as he shot to his feet to cheer, his elbow digging into my side on his way back into his seat.

But it got way, way worse. I'd finally managed to pinpoint Alfie once more, watching as he skillfully darted around one of the opposing players to grab the puck. With it practically glued to his stick, he raced down one side of the ice. He was heading towards the other team's goal when it happened.

Another player came out of the blue. His barrel-chest slammed into Alfie, sending him careening into the boards.

My heart jumped up into my throat as my stomach turned itself over. For an instant, I thought I was going to be sick. Even though there was no way the sound could carry all the way to our seats, I imagined the crunch of body against body.

I imagined Alfie's face twisted with pain.

Why would anybody willingly watch this level of violence?

With my fingers clenched on the edge of my seat, I leaned forward. With all my heart, I willed Alfie to be okay. To skate away from this miraculously unscathed.

But I didn't get my wish.

They had to help Alfie off the ice, taking him to have a medical check. I hated that I couldn't run back there to be with him. He wouldn't even have his phone on so that I could call to ask if he was okay.

After that, I simply couldn't stomach watching the rest of the game. It was too upsetting. I never wanted to see anybody get hurt, but especially not Alfie.

Making my apologies to Nadine, I promised her I'd get an Uber home. Even fighting my way out of the stadium was difficult. It wasn't until I made it outside that I could take an easy breath.

And even then, my stomach clenched with anxiety about Alfie. I sent him a text, which he didn't receive. It made me wonder if they'd let him back onto the ice. Maybe, at this moment, Alfie was getting hurt even worse.

I couldn't even stand to watch the rest of the game on the TV. I buried myself in my newest cookbook for the rest of the evening, only looking up when Nadine returned home to change before the party.

"You do still want to come, right?" she asked me anxiously. "Because this might be my only chance to really meet the Pumas!"

Pushing aside the sick feeling in my stomach, I nodded. "Of course," I agreed. Mostly, I wanted to see Alfie, to make sure he was okay. But of course, I couldn't tell Nadine that was my main motivation.

Chapter Nine

Alfie

It wasn't our finest game and that kind of sucked. Not playing our best was always shit but this time, knowing that Maya was in the audience, it made me want to play better. And for part of the game I did, but then an unfortunate check slammed me into the boards, my shoulder instantly aching.

For the rest of the game, I ended up watching from our doctor's office, icing my shoulder. Despite my insistence that I could go back out, he wasn't having any of it. We did still win, but it wasn't a game any of us would look back on with much pride.

Some games were just like that, I knew, but it would have been nice if this one hadn't been.

Then again, I had no idea if Maya even cared for hockey. It wasn't something that had come up. To me, it was difficult to imagine anyone not liking hockey. Even now, with my shoulder aching, I would have happily rushed out on the ice to play alongside my team.

Afterward, once I'd got equal amounts of concern and chirping for my shoulder, we did our usual interviews. There were a few questions to me about how my shoulder was doing. I was lucky, I told them, because it seemed unlikely that I'd have to miss any games.

The questions unexpectedly turned to *Serves You Right* and Maya. My answers were as PR-friendly as I could make them, probably borderline boring if the journalists' reactions were anything to go on.

"Check out our resident celebrity," Levi chirped after the media had left.

Rolling my eyes, I went about stripping my uniform off. The others, though, joined in. They teased me about how Maya and I had a hashtag and whether I'd be tattooing it on myself if we won.

"Oh, oh? Now we're thinking Alfie might win? After all the shit I got for being crap?" I asked.

"Well, you are still crap," Chuck pointed out.

"Yeah." Olle nodded from across the room. "Maya, however, we like."

There was nothing to say against that, to be fair. Maya was definitely worth liking. "Well, then you're in luck," I informed them all. "I invited her to the party at Luke's tonight." Our captain was very good at organizing parties for us, though it was a blessing it wasn't coming after a loss.

The guys seemed pleased with that and I made sure Maya had the address before leaving.

I had to make a quick detour home to pick up a couple of video games that the guys wanted to try out, which meant that by the time I got there, the party was off to a great start. My arrival was met with a cheer, though it was almost definitely more dedicated to the games I threw towards the guys.

Leaving them to it, I went through to the kitchen to get myself a drink. Checking my phone, I made sure that Maya was already here. Apparently, her cousin was midway through a conversation with Chase's girlfriend in the backyard, so I sent Maya a picture of me in the kitchen.

Best come rescue me before I start trying to cook, I sent with a grin tugging against the corners of my mouth.

It took a while before Maya appeared in the doorway. I'd used the time to pour myself a beer and grab a handful of snacks to keep me going. I hadn't expended as much energy in the game as I would have if I'd played the whole thing, but answering media questions was certainly thirsty work.

As soon as she saw me, Maya rushed forward. "Are you okay?" she asked, a note of genuine breathlessness in her voice. "I mean, you must be okay if you're here and you're texting me, but -"

She faltered, sucking her lower lip until it practically disappeared. "I couldn't stay and watch, not after you got hurt like that."

Her concern was sweet but it made me frown at first. There was still an ache in my shoulder and I was meant to ice it again in a bit, but truthfully, I'd already forgotten about the injury. It wasn't very serious.

The fact that Maya had left the game because of it made me instantly feel bad. She'd missed out on the game because of me. Kind of, at least.

"Oh, I'm fine," I assured her. "It wasn't very serious. Just needs some ice and a bit of a rest. Sorry you worried! I would have texted you earlier had I realized." And it struck me that that was true. Maya's concern for me was sweet but it made me feel bad, like I needed to reassure her.

Maya just frowned right back at me, her eyes narrowed and the cutest wrinkle appearing on the bridge of her nose.

"It looked serious," she informed me. "I knew that hockey was, well, quite aggressive, but I just couldn't watch when it was somebody that I knew."

She glanced away, almost as if she were embarrassed. "Nadine says I'm a wimp for not being able to handle it."

That made me give a surprised chuckle. The fact that her cousin had told Maya she was a wimp seemed somehow hilarious. While I obviously knew that hockey could be aggressive, it was so far down on the list of things that hockey was to me that I didn't even think about it. But I could see why Maya would.

"Maybe you're a bit of a wimp," I agreed and then laughed at the look Maya shot me. I raised my hands in mock surrender and then winced when it made pain shoot through my shoulder. "Just a little." The clarification didn't seem to really make her feel better.

Shaking my head, I shrugged, making sure to do so with my good shoulder. "It's part of the game, but it's not *the* game, you know? A bit of a risk, sure, but worth it, if you ask me."

Maya's expression didn't clear. "How can it possibly be *worth it*?" she asked. "There are so many sports where you don't have to get hurt, or at least where nobody is actively trying to hurt you."

The guy who'd checked me hadn't done it because he wanted to hurt me, but before I could explain that, Maya had carried on.

"I'm sorry. I know that you love it. It just doesn't really make sense to me."

Her apology made me pause. Obviously, to me, hockey was great. I even felt like it should be great for everyone. But I also knew that Maya felt like that about food. We were definitely different there.

"Food doesn't make sense to me," I shrugged. "So we're even?" I suggested.

Maybe it did bother me a little that Maya didn't like hockey. It was kind of hard to imagine her not liking something that mattered to me so much, but...

"Why did you come? To see the game?"

She could have just not and yeah, she had left, but that was because she'd watched me get hurt.

My heart quickened its beats in my chest, my stomach twisting slightly in a way that almost instantly made me want to smile.

She paused, toying with the hem of her shirt in a way that drew my gaze instantly to the flash of taut stomach.

It hit me unexpectedly that Maya had dressed up for the party. This wasn't her usual outfit of jeans and a t-shirt. The skirt she wore was clingy, wrapping around her hips, accentuating the curve of them.

Suddenly, my whole body felt hot.

"I wanted to support you, I suppose," she answered, reminding me that I'd asked her a question. "I thought maybe it would be different, watching it and wanting you to win. When I've tried to watch matches with Nadine, I've never cared about who scored more goals."

Maya smiled. "And it was different, but it was also horrible. I was so worried you'd be *hurt*."

For a moment, her words took my breath away.

I knew that my team cared about me getting hurt, of course. We all cared about each other, not to mention that it also hurt the team for any one of us to get injured and be sent off. And yes, that wasn't the primary reason my teammates didn't want me to get hurt, but it definitely played a part.

The fans didn't want me to get hurt either. Somewhat for similar reasons.

The management, too.

But Maya's concern came without anything else.

Well, she probably wanted me to be able to compete in *Serves You Right*, but I had absolutely no doubt that it hadn't even occurred to her as a concern.

No, Maya cared that I didn't get hurt. She just did.

And it took my breath away a little, because I was certain that, since my nana died, no one had cared about that for no other reason than just not wanting to see me be hurt. It felt almost overwhelming. I tried to hide those feelings behind the sip of my beer, shaking my head slightly.

"I promise, I'm not hurt. Well, I'm a little hurt. But nothing that's worth worrying about. You can hold some frozen peas against my shoulder if you want?" I joked, hoping it'd make the knot in my stomach unravel.

But Maya's soft giggle only made my muscles tense even further. It was such a sexy sound, like nothing I'd ever heard from her before.

"Do you even eat peas?" she asked, and I had to shake my head. Not that my distaste for vegetables would matter when it came to the benefits of icing an injury.

Maya seemed to disagree. "I've got frozen raspberries at home," she offered, clearly teasing, "we'll have to use them, instead."

"Luke's allergic to a whole bunch of stuff, but I bet even he and El have some frozen peas in their freezer," I commented, walking over to the freezer. It wasn't actually until I had retrieved a bag of frozen peas that it occurred to me exactly what Maya had said.

Turning around, I frowned. "I probably should have picked the raspberries, hmm?" Was Maya flirting? I found myself kind of hoping so. Walking back over, I held the bag of peas out to her. "So? Will you ice me?"

Maya's lips parted a little, like she was surprised this conversation wasn't entirely hypothetical. I had no idea whether that made it more or less likely that she'd been flirting.

It didn't matter, not when Maya whipped a dish towel off its hanger to wrap around the bag of frozen peas. My heart pounded harder at the thought of her coming closer, of her touching me - even if there would be layers of clothes and cloth and frozen vegetables between us.

"Where does it hurt?" she asked, with an amazing amount of gentleness in her voice.

The chatter from the party felt like it was in a different universe, not just a different room. Having Maya stand so close, all of my senses focused on her. Somehow, Maya seemed to be in more color than I had ever seen her before. It was like going from a grey day into a sunny one.

"Here," I drew out, brushing my hand over the top of my shoulder. "It's a bit achy still." Which it was and I actually was meant to ice it. What I probably was not meant to do was have Maya help me. It felt a bit like walking along the edge of a cliff, one where all it would take was a strong gust of wind and I'd fall.

Maya had to tiptoe up to hold the cold bag against the curve of my shoulder. I almost reached out a hand to steady her, but quickly pulled it back. If I touched the curve of her waist, I wasn't sure that I'd be able to stop.

"Does this kind of thing happen a lot?" Maya asked. "You never seem to be sore at filming, just tired sometimes."

"I don't get hurt like this a lot," I told her, my tone almost a promise. Knowing now that Maya worried, that she didn't want me hurt, it made me want to reassure her that I wasn't hurt often. It was mostly true, too. I'd been lucky with the injuries throughout my career.

As for not seeming to be sore, that probably was less accurate.

"Training can leave me sore, games are easier because of the adrenaline." It wasn't actually something I thought much about, but that was probably because no one had asked me these sorts of questions. "It's just part of my job. You must get tired after catering big events?"

Maya shifted the peas a little, the cold slowly weaving through the ache, lifting it out of me. I gave a soft sigh, so close that Maya's glossy hair shivered as the air moved between us.

"Oh, of course," she agreed. "And my feet ache, even when I wear comfortable shoes. And sometimes I catch myself on the knife, you saw how clumsy I was at the skipping."

She paused, realization dawning in her eyes. "Oh. I see. I don't mind any of that, because cooking for people is what I want to do more than anything."

It made me smile, both at the fact that she seemed to get what I meant but also that I'd managed to explain it in a way she understood. Explaining things wasn't exactly something I thought I was great at, but I wanted Maya to get it. To get me.

"Yeah." I nodded, my tongue darting out to wet my lips. "Sometimes the aches and pains are worth it. And sure, maybe you don't have to ice your shoulders, but I very rarely almost lose a finger," I teased.

She giggled, looking up at me with amusement. "I hardly ever do that anymore," she promised, making me smile. In that moment, all the differences between us seemed to disappear.

Maya might not like hockey, and I might not like vegetables, but we both understood the other's passion, even if we didn't share it.

Her fingers brushed against the side of my neck, sending an electric shiver down my spine.

My gaze dropped to her lips and I leaned forward almost without a second thought, my nose bumping against the softness of her cheek.

In my chest, my heart was pounding so hard that I couldn't help but wonder if Maya could feel it through the bag of peas against my shoulder. This time, my hand did come up to settle against her hip. Everything felt like it was happening in slow motion. She moved forward, leaning a little bit into me.

And then a couple of the guys came in.

Maya and I instantly sprang apart. From the laughter and chirping going on, I was sure none of them had seen anything. Not that there had been something to see, right? Maya was just... helping me.

Ah. Well.

I was so screwed.

"Oh, Maya!" Chuck exclaimed when he spotted us. "We know you from the TV! You've been doing so great at making sure the guys who bet for Alfie to go out in the first week lost," he informed her, making a couple of the other guys chuckle.

I rolled my eyes. "Guys like you, you mean?"

"It's not just me," Maya insisted, reminding me all over again that she didn't really understand the way we hockey players teased each other. I hoped that, by actually getting to meet some of them, she'd see that it wasn't as mean-spirited as it might sound.

But she bravely carried on, "Alfie's really helpful in the kitchen. He doesn't argue with me like some of the other celebrities do."

Chuck shook his head, like he couldn't quite believe it. And I couldn't even blame him. I wouldn't have believed I could be 'helpful in the kitchen' a few weeks ago.

Handing me the bag of peas, Maya touched the back of her free hand to her cheek, like she was trying to cool it.

"I should make sure Nadine's alright," she said softly to me.

Not being around Maya for a bit was probably best for both of us. The heat that had radiated from Maya stood in such contrast to how cool my shoulder felt. It was impossible not to wish to reach out again, to brush my hand over her back, to pull her in closer...

But that couldn't happen.

Even as much as had happened shouldn't have.

"Sure." I nodded, trying not to let my mind wander. Maya had stepped in closer, she'd tilted her head, those weren't things that I had imagined. But we weren't supposed to do this, it was bad enough that there were rumors about us.

After Maya left, the guys easily fell into chirping me about even being in a kitchen, calling it my natural habitat now. It was easy enough to take. Before long, I had managed to distract them with conversation about the video games. That, of course, then led to us playing some.

It was a few hours later, once my head and body had stopped aching for Maya that I went to find her again. With her cousin being there, I didn't feel too bad for not checking in sooner, but only barely. It was still me who'd invited her here.

As it turned out, I hadn't really needed to worry. Maya had found El and the two were discussing food. It made Maya's whole face light up, making it impossible for me to look away.

"Oh, there he is," El nodded towards me and my eyes widened.

"Me?" Though she obviously had meant me.

"Yeah, you," El laughed. "Maya needs a ride home. Nadine's, ah, Nadine and Chuck seem to have hit it off pretty well, if you get my drift." She grinned and Maya's cheeks reddened.

"Oh." I guess that was nice for Chuck. But also nice for me, since it gave me more of an opportunity to spend time with Maya. Whether that was a good idea, I wasn't actually too sure.

Still, of course, I gave her a ride home. Parking outside Maya's apartment building, I tried not to look at her. The car ride had been pretty quiet, like both of us worried we might just say the wrong thing.

I was about to say thanks for coming to the game and the party when Maya asked if I wanted to come upstairs. For a coffee.

It could have, really, been for anything.
The answer would have always been yes.

Chapter Ten

Maya

My whole body vibrated with excitement as I led Alfie up the stairs to my apartment. We'd come so close to making out in the kitchen at the party, and I couldn't seem to chase the desire out of the corners of my mind.

Knowing that we shouldn't only made it worse. The phrase 'forbidden love' had never really meant anything to me until now. I'd never understood all those stories of people who risked everything to be together.

Not that I was going to risk everything. My intentions shifted second by second. One moment, I wanted nothing more than to press Alfie against the door as soon as I got him inside. The next, I knew better than to throw away all the good that *Serves You Right* could potentially do for my career.

Alfie was unreadable. Getting disqualified from the show wouldn't mean anything to him, so it wasn't fair to rely on him to hold us back.

More than anything, I wanted to know what Alfie was thinking. I knew he was attracted to me, our almost-kiss in the kitchen had proved that. But whether Alfie wanted one night or something more serious was a total mystery.

And I couldn't risk disqualification if it was just sex. I'd regret it forever. It would be different if Alfie and I were meant to be something more than cooking competition partners.

But I had no idea how to ask him.

"So, this is my kitchen," I said, as I pushed open the door. It was small, of course, but Nadine let me have the majority of the storage. I had my own set of chef's knives, a hand mixer, and a countertop pizza oven that had been a somewhat impractical gift from my parents.

"I'll make you the best cup of coffee you've ever had," I promised, getting out my stovetop coffee maker.

When Alfie took a seat across the counter from me, I was equal parts relieved and disappointed. I wasn't sure what I was expecting, though, and whatever it was, I almost definitely shouldn't have been expecting it.

"That is a very daring promise," he informed me, but a smile played on Alfie's lips that informed me that he believed that I could achieve it. The way Alfie seemed to support me so unconditionally, despite hardly knowing me, made my heart skip a beat.

"Is it?" I teased. "No offense, Alfie, but you don't seem like you'd be the most adventurous coffee drinker in the world." I'd be a little surprised if Alfie had even had coffee other than from Starbucks.

But, he did earn a lot of money as an NHL player, so maybe I was wrong. "Do you get to travel a lot?" I asked. Traveling was what I would do if I had a lot of money. Well, once I'd set up my own catering firm, anyway.

"Rude," Alfie laughed and my eyes widened. It hadn't been my intention to be rude in saying that I didn't think he'd know good coffee. My face must have shown my worry, because Alfie shook his head. "I'm joking. It's a fair observation," he promised. "Probably accurate, too."

"Is that why you ask about traveling? To see my world knowledge of coffee? I've traveled a bit," he answered. "Obviously, for work, but for fun, too. Levi and I have been traveling for a few summers now. We did Chile last summer, hoping to do Europe this summer. How about you?"

"That sounds cool," I said, trying to squash down the flicker of envy that I felt. "I'd love to travel with a friend. I've only ever been on vacation with my parents when I was a kid."

Not that there was anything wrong with family vacations. "I imagine it's pretty different to go with someone your own age."

Once I'd filled the coffee maker, I set it carefully on the stovetop, taking a seat on the other side of the counter.

"I'd love to go to Europe," I added. "Have you thought about where you want to go?"

"Olle wants us to come to Sweden, but I think we'll probably start with Italy," Alfie answered. I remembered briefly chatting to Olle at the party so I knew he was Swedish. It made sense he'd want to have his friends visit.

"Where did you go?" The question made me frown, unsure what Alfie meant. "With your parents," he explained. "Where did you go? I've never been on a holiday with my family, it sounds... Well, I suppose it depends on the family," he frowned.

"We went to Canada a few times," I answered. "Banff National Park, and Prince Edward Island. They're both beautiful. We did a bus tour of waterfalls and saw a baby black bear, that was pretty spectacular."

I shrugged slightly. "It was nice, but we always did the things my parents wanted, not necessarily things I would have chosen." After all, not only were they older and, supposedly, wiser, there were also two of them and one of me.

"But I'm not complaining," I rushed to add. "I know I was lucky to go on vacations at all." Plenty of people didn't have that luxury.

Alfie gave a small hum. His thoughts were drifting off somewhere, but it didn't seem right to ask where. If Alfie wanted me to know, I was sure he'd tell me.

"So where's your coffee talent from?" Alfie asked instead. It was an obvious change of subject but I let him lead. Now was not the right time to push. Instead, I got up again to check on the coffee, giving Alfie a smile over my shoulder. It was sweet that he already called it a talent without having even tasted the promised coffee.

I chuckled. "I've spent years working with chefs, Alfie," I point out. "The only thing we love almost as much as cooking is eating and drinking."

My memory wasn't good enough to recall which of my colleagues had recommended the stovetop coffee maker as absolutely revolutionary, but they had been totally right.

And then, on top of that, someone had recommended the best ground coffee in Salt Lake City, from a tiny store that sold it in densely-packed bags.

Pouring out the dark liquid, I inhaled appreciatively. "Milk?" I asked. "Sugar?"

"I'll try it black first," Alfie decided. "Then probably milk." He almost sounded apologetic, which made me laugh. I wasn't going to judge Alfie for putting milk in his coffee. I might be a bit of a foodie, but I wasn't that bad.

Handing Alfie the cup, our fingers brushed briefly. The touch didn't linger like it had back at the party, but it still lasted a bit longer than absolutely necessary. Neither of us said anything, though. Instead, Alfie brought the cup up to his lips.

I found myself holding my breath, as if his verdict deserved the anticipation. And maybe it did. Watching him take a sip, I could practically hear my heart beat. Why it suddenly mattered so much to know what Alfie made of my coffee, I had no idea.

And yet, it did.

So when he smiled, it allowed me to give a sigh of relief.

"It's good!" he promised. "Maybe even better than good. Kind of... nutty? Oh, God, do I now have opinions about tastes and flavors?"

I laughed aloud, my smile so wide that I could feel it in my cheeks. "Everyone has opinions about tastes and flavors," I told him. "It's innate. I think that's kind of what I love about it."

His expression clearly encouraged me to carry on, so I did, trying not to feel self-conscious about the passion I couldn't completely hide.

"You can't fake good food. And you can't control what tastes you like. It's not like a film or a piece of music where you can see how it's good even if you don't like it. You either like how something tastes or you don't, and it doesn't matter whether it was technically well-cooked or not."

It made good cooking more of a challenge, but also something that was intensely personal. It was no good to be able to perfectly bone and grill a fillet of fish if the person you were cooking for didn't like the taste.

"I guess it's kind of like hockey," I added, surprising myself with the connection. "You can train for hours, but none of that matters if you don't score, right?"

Alfie gave a soft hum at that. "I suppose it depends what you mean by matters," he said, shrugging. "I love the game. I guess, maybe how you love to cook?" The suggestion earned a soft nod from me. Even if I had been awful at cooking, I probably would still enjoy the process. But it did help being good at it.

Taking another sip of his coffee, Alfie set the cup down. "It's good. You're very good at making things," he told me, the tone soft.

I wished I could return the compliment, say that Alfie was very good at playing hockey. But I hadn't even stayed to watch the end of the game. Even if I had, I didn't know bad hockey-playing from good.

"And you're very brave," I said instead. That much was very true. "Not just because you play hockey, but also because you came on the show when you didn't think you could cook. And you did your best to help me."

I licked my lips, suddenly wanting to lean forward and capture Alfie's mouth with my own. He'd made so much effort, and I knew that it was because he didn't want to let me down. Nobody had ever cared so much about my dreams. I wished I could explain that in a way Alfie would understand.

"I'm not sure it's brave," Alfie shook his head. "More like dumb," he teased. I didn't point out that the line between brave and stupid was pretty thin. Still, it was hard to imagine doing *Serves You Right* with anyone else.

Truthfully, part of what made *Serves You Right* so much fun was Alfie. There was no one else who would have jumped with me just to get me to do a jump rope challenge, I was sure.

The silence that fell felt companionable. We drank our coffee, shooting soft smiles over the rim of our cups at each other. When Alfie's cup was empty, he stood up to take it over to the sink, but rather than returning to his seat, Alfie stopped by mine.

"About earlier," he drew out, but no other words followed.

Instead, Alfie's hand reached out, fingers soft as they brushed over my cheek.

I shivered, heat blooming from his touch. "You don't have to say anything," I breathed.

Even as I said the words, I wondered whether it would be better if we *did* talk about it. If we could say, out loud, that we knew it couldn't happen again, we were less likely to give in to temptation.

But I didn't *want* it to be less likely.

Swallowing, I pulled away a little. "This competition is really important to me," I said softly, even though there was no doubt Alfie already knew that.

"Yeah," he breathed. For a moment, I was so sure that Alfie would say to just screw it. To throw the competition out of the window. Or even just to lie. Was that what I wanted him to say? I had no idea. I could barely put a thought together.

Instead, all of my focus was on Alfie. He was so close that the smell of his cologne enveloped me. It made me want to lean in, to tilt my head up and seek his lips out with mine.

I even closed my eyes, so sure that a kiss would come.

But it didn't.

Alfie pulled his hand back, moving away just far enough that the warmth of his body left me. My breath caught, eyes opening to blink up at Alfie.

"I'm sorry, this is... I should go."

The words wrenched my heart out of my chest. But I knew Alfie was right. The chemistry between us wasn't enough of a reason to risk everything.

And until we knew whether it was more than just chemistry, we had to hold back.

I nodded, forcing myself to smile, though I was sure it didn't look genuine.

"Thank you." In my muddled mind, I hardly knew what it was that I was grateful for. But I trusted Alfie, believed that his intentions were good.

If they hadn't been, he would have let me lead us straight into temptation.

"I'll see you at filming?" That was several days away; maybe some time apart would help to cool things down.

For a moment, I was sure Alfie was about to say 'fuck it' and kiss me anyway. But it was almost possible to see the thoughts return, the knowledge that we shouldn't coming back. He gave a small nod.

"Yes, of course," he promised easily. The tone was back to that familiar, friendly way Alfie normally spoke to me. A few steps back and that was it, we were once again just partners on a cooking show. And if my heart tugged a little at the idea of being a real-life #alfaya? Well, I needed to get over that.

Alfie's tongue darted out to wet his lips and I had to glance away. "Thanks for coming to see the game and for helping me with my shoulder," Alfie said. "I'll... yeah. Filming. See you then."

I smiled, not wanting him to go but knowing it was for the best. After all, if things between us were really meant to be, who knew what would happen when we finally wrapped up filming *Serves You Right* for good?

The thought that maybe this wasn't saying 'no' forever helped me send Alfie away without too much pain.

Maybe it wasn't sensible to console myself with thoughts of what could happen *after* we were released from our non-fraternization contract. But sensible or not, I couldn't seem to stop my mind from going there.

It was better than nothing. That helped me push aside the pang of regret in my chest as I peered out my window to watch Alfie getting into his car and driving away.

Chapter Eleven

Alfie

The next day, training was optional, like it always was after a game. With my shoulder still aching, I probably should have stayed home, but my mind kept spinning around what had happened last night. Or rather, what hadn't happened.

The warmth of Maya's body still lingered against my hands. Part of me deeply regretted not having kissed her, even if I knew that what I should be regretting is how close I'd come to breaking our non-fraternization contract.

Those thoughts kept spinning in my head over and over again, all the possibilities flashing before me. But also the knowledge that I didn't actually believe those were all the possibilities.

Whatever it was, I needed it out of my head.

A morning skate seemed a pretty good remedy. Then, after being checked over by the team's doctor again, I headed to the gym. They told me not to overuse my shoulder but I hardly needed it for some cycling.

Not a lot of the guys had come to the optional skate, which was understandable. But both Chuck and Chase somewhat unexpectedly joined me at the gym. They were chatting about some nonsense when the advert for *Serves You Right* flashed up on the TV screen before us.

"Oh, look, it's our resident celebrity and his cute girlfriend," Chuck laughed.

Yesterday, it might have been easy to dismiss that, but today the words cut deeper. I couldn't tell the guys about what had happened. Especially when nothing had actually happened.

"You know they can kick us off the show for that, right?" I asked instead.

"What?" Chase asked. "Why?"

Honestly, I didn't have an answer for that. When I'd initially signed the contract, the idea that I might want to date anyone on the show hadn't even entered my head. It wasn't as if I dated a lot, so the chances that one of the few people I'd be interested in would also be appearing on *Serves You Right* hadn't seemed high.

"What about after the show finishes filming?" Chuck added. "Surely they can't keep you from doing whatever - or whoever - you want once you're done with the episodes?"

"No, I guess not." I shrugged like I hadn't already thought about that. I definitely had. But I had no idea how long this would go on, whether we'd have to do press for a while after and if that still counted as being on the show.

More importantly, though, I had no idea if Maya would still be interested in me. Or if she was interested in me now. Yes, we definitely had... chemistry. But that didn't mean she was interested in dating me. Not to mention that we didn't have a lot in common.

Maya didn't like hockey and I didn't... well, I suppose I liked some food. Maya loved food, though. It wasn't a passion I even understood much less shared.

"Anyway, just because social media ships us or whatever doesn't mean there's something there," I informed them dismissively.

"Why not?" Chase asked, his tone almost challenging. "She's gorgeous, she's clearly talented if she's managed to keep your inept ass on the show for this long. What is there not to like?"

If Chase hadn't been absolutely committed to his girlfriend Morgan, I might've felt a little jealous. I didn't want anyone else noticing how gorgeous Maya was, or how talented.

"And it looked like she was into you," Chuck added. "We barely got a chance to talk to her at the party because you kept her all to yourself."

Neither of those observations were wrong, of course. It was difficult to deny that I did like Maya. But if anything, she was probably too good for me. Not that I planned to tell that to Chase and Chuck.

"Just... we don't have a lot in common," I said, shrugging. That wasn't even a lie. Sure, maybe we shared some sexual tension. I did think Maya was cute and I tried very hard not to think about how good she'd felt in my arms. But none of that would matter if we found ourselves having nothing to share outside of that.

Chuck snorted, but Chase gave a thoughtful hum. He and Morgan were pretty similar. She liked racing and he liked hockey, but they were both thrill-seekers, so they definitely had common ground.

"Yeah, I guess I can see how that would be a problem," he admitted. "I mean, she probably does a lot of cooking for whoever she's dating, right? Like El does for Luke."

Luke was hard to cook for, with all his different allergies, but El had joked that I was harder. Maybe Maya wouldn't want to cook for someone who didn't like any of the ingredients she did.

The thought made me sad. It was the first time I'd ever thought I might be *missing out* by refusing to eat vegetables.

But just because I liked Maya didn't mean I was going to like vegetables.

It would be disappointing, right? For her? To cook for someone like me. She was so good with it now, always trying to make something at the competition that I would try. Surely no one wanted that as a forever thing.

When I didn't say anything, Chuck frowned at me. "Does it bother you? The whole #alfaya thing?"

"No." I shook my head. "I mean, it's not like I'm insulted to have people think I'd be interested in someone like Maya. Mostly, I just worry about the show getting the wrong idea. Though, they probably love the publicity."

There was no way I'd risk getting Maya disqualified.

"I wouldn't worry about that part of it," Chase assured me. "I mean, they always want there to be gossip, right? As long as they don't actually catch you doing anything you shouldn't be, you'll be fine."

Temptation fluttered inside me. After all, even if I had kissed Maya in her apartment, there was no way the show would find out about it - unless one of us told them.

But it was better to be safe. Especially when it was Maya's future on the line. She'd said herself how great an opportunity the show was for her. I couldn't be the one to ruin it.

"Or you could always flirt with someone else," Chuck suggested. "The singer, Michelle? She's pretty too."

"Maxine," I corrected automatically before frowning slightly. I liked Maxine a lot, but ever since the competition had started, I'd viewed her more as a friend than anything else. The idea of flirting with her felt kind of weird.

But it did make me realize how little attention I paid to anyone but Maya on set. There were other beautiful women there, Alix for example, or Didi. They were attractive, sure, but a voice somewhere at the back of my head added that, despite their attractiveness, they weren't Maya.

Shaking my head, I cycled more intensely on my bike. "It doesn't really matter. Maya and I, we're not, you know. Nothing's going on."

Chase and Chuck seemed to accept that. My heart pounded harder against my ribs, and I wasn't sure whether it was the cycling, or the fear that they might suggest I set Maya up with someone else.

After all, a lot of the Pumas were still single and looking for girlfriends. It wouldn't have been rare for someone to suggest that one of them might be interested in Maya, since I wasn't.

Chuck and Nadine had already hit it off.

Despite my fears, neither of them said anything. It was hard to tell whether that was comforting or just a sign that they didn't really believe my protests that there was nothing going on.

They'd have been right to think I was lying to them. And that made me feel bad, too.

"Don't you ever want a girlfriend?" Chase asked me suddenly. "I can't even remember when you last went out on a date."

I gave a small shrug.

Chase wasn't wrong, it had been ages since I'd even been on a date. It wasn't that I didn't like it or anything, but getting attached to someone just led to losing them. I wasn't very interested in that. Even with Maya, as much as I liked her, there was a risk that things just wouldn't work out and the idea of missing her felt worse than not having her in the first place.

"Sure," I answered finally. "But we're busy with games and stuff. I'd rather have a Stanley Cup than a girlfriend." I grinned, knowing that the guys would agree, even Chase who did have a girlfriend.

They laughed, Chuck going so far as to pound my back in passing. It knocked the wind out of me, making it impossible to say anything for several seconds.

Chase gave a mournful sigh. "I want to say it's possible to have both, but I haven't managed it yet," he admitted, making Chuck roll his eyes.

"Enough talk of girls," he decided. "Come on, I want a turn on the bike. Are you almost done, Alfie?"

I was glad for the change of topic, easily letting Chuck take over. We decided to compete, of course, which distracted everyone from talking or thinking about Maya. It was what I had needed all along, the distraction serving me well.

Of course, by the time I was heading home, the memories of yesterday were slowly creeping back in. They didn't feel as raw, though, or as urgent. Maybe I could do this, just keep things platonic between Maya and me.

The talk had reminded me of the reasons I didn't date anyway. And also of all the reasons I couldn't date Maya.

We weren't compatible, our interests and lifestyles were so different.

Maybe if I focused on that, it'd be easier to not want her.

~*~

It wasn't until the following week that Maya and I saw each other again. The time, I had hoped, would put more of a distance between us, but the moment I saw Maya that day, I knew it hadn't worked. Not for me, anyway. My heart skipped a beat at the way she smiled at me.

Our conversation before the filming started was a bit awkward, but not so much that anyone else would notice. Mostly just a bit stilted. Thankfully, the filming started with a new challenge being explained to us.

This week, Didi told us, we were going to cook our favorite childhood foods. We had to adapt them to be suitable for an adult dinner party, which thankfully was almost definitely more of a task for Maya than me. If it was me, they would all just be eating chicken nuggets.

"So," I said once the task had been explained and we'd moved to our cooking stations. "What are you thinking?" Because I knew with confidence that Maya would already be thinking of something.

"My first thought was birthday cake," Maya admitted. "I only ever had store-bought ones as a kid, but there's something special about somebody making a whole cake just to celebrate the fact that you exist, you know?"

I hadn't thought about it that way, but I could see what Maya meant. Like Christmas, the excitement of waking up the morning of your birthday when you were little was unlike anything in adult life.

"But what about you?" Maya asked. "We can't just do my favorite food, we have to find a way to do yours, too."

"Um..." I hesitated. Cake was an awesome choice, definitely more interesting than the many different easy-to-cook things I'd had as a kid. My nana had often been working, so she left me at home with things I could just put in the oven or heat up in the microwave.

Thinking about how much of that I wanted to disclose on camera, I gave a small shrug. "Pizza?" I offered. When Maya frowned, I shrugged. "I grew up with just my nana," I explained. "And she was often busy working, you know? So... pizza was easy. Basically, if it was easy to cook, that's what we ate."

After a moment, I glanced at the cameras. Part of what the celebrity winner would get was a donation to help kids who struggled with obtaining food. Maybe...

"Could we do something easy? Something anyone could do at home?"

It was quite a big ask, when it also had to be suitable to serve at an adult dinner party. I almost expected Maya to say no the moment the question left my lips.

But she didn't. She screwed up her mouth, her whole face expressing how hard she was thinking. I didn't interrupt, wanting to give her as much time as she needed.

"What if we made pizza into little individual-sized pot pies?" Maya suggested. "We could make the dough ourselves, but anyone watching at home could use one of those kits that you just have to add water to. It would do the same job, I think."

Even I knew what she was referring to, so hope soared in me. "Yeah," I nodded. "Could we do that? I know it's not as... I guess advanced? As you can be. You're such a great chef, but it'd be nice to make something, well -" I shrugged a little sheepishly - "something even I could make."

Maybe if a kid saw us do it, it'd be easier for them to try to make something. To know that other people had experiences like what I'd had probably would have helped me as a kid.

"Maya," Didi called from behind the cameras. "Ask Alfie more about his childhood," she instructed, making me frown. It must have shown, because Didi rushed in to clarify. "It's topical, don't be shy. A lot of people would love to hear about you growing up."

Maya paused; I couldn't blame her. It was weird to be told what we should talk about, there was no way to move naturally back into the conversation.

Her shoulders lifted slightly, as if she were sighing but not quite doing it out loud. "What were mealtimes like?" she asked. "Did your nana sit and eat with you?"

Since we were supposed to be talking about me, Maya handed me an onion and a knife without any verbal instructions. I could figure out what she wanted from that, at least.

"Sometimes," I answered after a moment. Knowing that this was something that Didi felt would make good TV felt awkward, but if I pushed myself not to focus on that, it became a bit easier.

For a moment, I tried to just think about what I was willing to talk about so publicly. It wasn't like I was ashamed of my upbringing, far from it. And if I was going to share it with someone, Maya was a great person to pick.

Well, Maya and whoever watched *Serves You Right*.

"When I was four, my nana took over caring for me. Mom wasn't... in a position to raise me and I never knew my dad. My nana took on bringing me up and she was great. But she had to work a lot to support me, especially when I started playing hockey. So often she had to work, but when she didn't, nana was usually too tired to make anything too complicated, so pizza was a big favorite."

Maya nodded, white teeth nipping into her full lower lip. I wished we could be having this conversation in private, where I wouldn't have to worry about what to divulge, and Maya wouldn't have to wonder whether her reaction was the right one.

It must be even harder for her. At least I was used to the press asking invasive questions.

"Pizza's good," she agreed. I could almost see Didi's underwhelmed eye-roll. Maya must have sensed it, because she carried on.

"No, I mean - well, my mom used to feed me pizza, too. She would sit with me while I ate, and then cook something later for her and my dad, once he got home from work."

It was my turn to frown. From what Maya had told me about her love of food, it very much involved people. That's why she liked catering rather than just cooking. A sense of a community, she'd said. But eating while your mom watched and knowing she then cooked something else for herself? It didn't sound like it fit in that narrative.

"It sounds kind of lonely," I commented before I could stop myself. When the realization hit me of how harsh that must sound, my eyes widened. "Sorry! Maybe not? I mean, I wouldn't know, I had loads of dinners on my own as a kid." Which was certainly true.

"No, it was," Maya agreed simply. "I think my mom did the best she could, because there was no way I could stay up late enough to eat with my dad. One of us was going to have to eat alone, and at least my mom sat with me, so I wasn't completely by myself."

When Maya put it that way, I could kind of understand it. If I ever had a girlfriend, I'd appreciate her waiting to eat with me when I got back from training.

"But when we'd go to my aunt's house for Christmas, or Thanksgiving, and there'd be all these cousins around..." Maya's whole face lit up as she spoke. "That was just the best feeling. And I think pizza's like that for a lot of people, you know? Something that you grab to feed your friends when they're helping you move house. Or at a party."

Her enthusiasm made me smile. It was impossible not to and I had to look down to make sure I didn't chop my fingers off while getting distracted by Maya. The way she talked about food, or rather, the way she talked about feeding people, it made me appreciate food in a way I honestly would have never known to.

"So we're going to do little pizzas," I nodded. "For all our childhood memories. And birthday cake. What do you want to do with the birthday cake? What's your best birthday cake experience?" Which was mostly asking her in a roundabout way what her best birthday had been.

"Probably my first one after I moved out here," she admitted, "but that's not really a childhood meal. It was only a few months ago!" We both laughed, Maya whipping up a dough so effortlessly that it made me appreciate just how much she actually knew about food. If it had been me, I'd have needed a recipe, and even then it might have gone wrong.

Maya's smile continued to light up her face. It was no surprise that the camera lingered on our counter. "Nadine took the day off work so that we could spend it together before my shift," she explained. "And, even though I do most of the cooking, she and Sophie made me a proper birthday cake."

It was sweet that Maya's friends had come together just to give her something special. But it didn't exactly inspire me with any ideas. "What about you? Did you ever have a hockey-themed cake?"

The question made me laugh. "Yes, actually, I did," I nodded. "On multiple occasions. More recently was a few years back. Levi and Chuck baked me a cake. It was awful and mostly just sponge, but the effort was great." Even if the cake had been mostly inedible, making it for me had been very sweet.

"Do you like birthday cakes because they are made to be shared?" I asked. Maya seemed to enjoy the coming together of people, the experiences that people got to have with each other.

Maya looked thoughtful for a moment, then nodded. "I think that's part of it, but also the effort that goes into making it. Somebody thought you were not only special enough that they spent hours making you something, but they also thought other people would want to celebrate you, too!"

If I looked at it that way, I could see what Maya meant.

"So, since we're doing individual pizza pot pies, maybe we need to make the sharing of the cake a feature," Maya suggested.

At first, I wasn't even sure what that meant. Luckily for me, Maya carried on. "You can make cupcakes that have a hidden stash of candy inside. I bet we could do that with a bigger cake, too. Then cutting into it to share it out becomes this big reveal moment."

"Oh!" I exclaimed as something occurred to me. "Wait, I have an idea," I told Maya before walking off set to get my phone. Didi told me off for it, of course, but it wasn't as if there weren't other people they could film. It served her right for pushing such intrusive questions.

When I returned, I was already putting the words in a search engine. "I saw this online," I told Maya, clicking on the right video. It showed a woman making cupcakes and then decorating them as an overall cake. "We could do that," I told Maya. "Make many cupcakes look like one cake? And the sweets, too. Do you... is that a good idea?"

In my excitement of thinking of an idea, I hadn't got as far as considering whether it was something Maya would think of as good.

My moment of stomach-churning anxiety was brief. Maya grinned, almost bouncing on the balls of her feet as she nodded her enthusiasm.

"Yes, Alfie, that's brilliant! And that way, it's another thing that people can do at home. They can buy a cupcake-making kit, or just unfrosted cupcakes from the grocery store.

I watched as Maya's eyes darted from her bowl to my chopping board. "Okay, we're going to need to get a move on. We've got no time to lose," she told me seriously.

As she gave me instructions on what to do, I couldn't help but glance at Maya, a smile playing on my lips. It felt good to make suggestions that she liked. It also, I realized, felt good to have talked to Maya about my childhood. Would I have picked to do it on camera? No, probably not. Definitely not. But it was still better than not having had that conversation at all.

The fondness I felt towards Maya, though, did little to stop me from wanting to reach out to her. I had hoped that the few days between us would squash the desire I felt for her. But as I watched her, out of the corner of my eye so I wouldn't make it obvious, there was no denying that an attraction was still there.

Maybe if I just tried harder.

Or didn't think about it.

Or something.

Chapter Twelve

Maya

Cooking had always been my favorite way to spend time. I'd had no idea that doing it *with* someone else could make it even better. And yet, when I worked with Alfie, both of us contributing ideas and building on our understanding of one another's childhoods, it lit me up inside like nothing before ever had.

Alfie might claim he couldn't cook, and maybe that was true in terms of him not knowing specific techniques, but he understood everything I said about food.

As we worked together, trading ingredients back and forth as I directed Alfie through the steps of the recipe, everything else faded. All I could think about was the dishes we'd decided on and how good it felt to have Alfie close at hand, handing me things that I needed, praising my quickness with the knife or my handling of the dough.

Time lost all meaning. Until the challenge timer buzzed to let us know we needed to get out plates up to the judges' table.

"Oh, my God," I breathed. "I think we actually did it." Alfie had just finished tossing the salad which would accompany our pizza pot-pie as I'd stuck candles into our cupcake cake. "Did we forget anything?" We hadn't lit the candles, of course, that could wait until they were ready to film the judges trying our food.

"Nope, I think we're good," Alfie announced with such a wide smile that my stomach flipped. He looked gorgeous. Not that he didn't look gorgeous anyway, but there was something extra about having him smile at me like that.

We had a break between finishing and the judging starting, during which we got to have a quick look at what everyone else had made. We seemed to be the only ones who'd gone for something simple, most of the others had made very elaborate dishes.

I had worried a little but Alfie's dramatic 'ours is better' whisper made me laugh. As it turned out, the judges agreed! They were impressed with us making something simple and keeping it easy enough for home cooks, but putting our own twist on it.

"And this tastes amazing," Lauren, one of the judges, informed us, reaching for another spoonful of our pizza.

If anything, Alfie's smile seemed to get even wider.

"Pizza's always popular," I commented, feeling my face flush slightly in the glare of the camera. "And it's so easy to customize them this way. You can cater to vegetarians, people with allergies. A dinner party shouldn't be stressful, for the cook or the guests."

Aaron and James had made a spicy peanut chicken stew, which would be a lot harder to adapt to varying tastes than our pizzas would be. Also, while peanut butter definitely was a childhood food, their choice in what they've made seemed a bit too unusual.

"Getting together for food should be fun, so we made foods that were suited to an adult palate but would still remind people of how enjoyable eating as a group can be."

"And, you know," Alfie shrugged. "We made it based on our childhood favorites. Maybe it's just my *terribly disadvantaged childhood*," he said mockingly, glaring at the camera. "But I don't remember peanut stew being very popular?" In fact, it wasn't very popular now either, given how many people were allergic to nuts.

I had to bite my lip not to grin. Alfie gave a small shrug. "Pizza and cake! Who doesn't love pizza and cake, right?"

And the judges agreed. They named us the best of the week, something I could hardly believe. We'd come above all the other amazing chefs there. Winning this week also meant that we were definitely moving into the next week, another successful week for Alfie and me.

In the end, it was Tex, the reality TV star, and his chef Christine who ended up being sent home. They had made some sort of a soup that the judges didn't think was very 'interesting'. I felt a bit bad, since our pizza and cake had somehow been more exciting, but not so bad that I wasn't also pleased.

Once we'd finished filming, and said our goodbyes to Christine and Tex, we moved to the backstage area to collect up our things. Despite how much I'd loved working with Alfie, it had been stressful to get both dishes finished in the time we'd been given.

I could feel the strain in my lower back, just beginning to ache. It made me sigh, but there was no sense complaining about it. When *Serves You Right* had confirmed that they wanted me as one of their chefs, I'd promised my boss that it wouldn't get in the way of work.

Which meant I couldn't make excuses about filming taking up all my energy and get away with it.

"What are you doing this evening?" I asked Alfie, hoping he might tell me about something exciting he had planned. I could live vicariously through him, even if all I had time for was work and more work.

Instead, Alfie gave a small shrug. "No real plans, honestly," he answered. "Maybe watch some TV, might invite a few of the guys over for video games, but I haven't set my heart on it yet." An evening off sounded so nice right now, but my next free night wasn't for days.

"What about you? Have you got anything fun planned?" Alfie asked. I realized I hadn't actually told him that where I was heading next was work rather than home.

"No," I answered, double-checking that I had everything I'd need for my shift. "We're catering at some corporate event. It doesn't start for another few hours, but I promised my boss I'd help unload the trucks."

Having to do more than my fair share of grunt work was definitely the downside of being the company's most junior chef. "They need someone to make sure all the food gets set up in the right order. No leaving the frozen desserts on the counter and putting the soup in the freezer."

You'd think it would be obvious, but mistakes had happened in the past.

"It's going to be a long night."

"Oh." Alfie frowned. "But aren't you already kind of tired? We've been making food for ages." Though, as he said it, Alfie seemed to realize that my tiredness wasn't exactly relevant. We both knew - and it was an interesting thing in its own right, being so sure that I knew Alfie well enough to think so - that if Alfie had training after we filmed, he'd still go.

As if reading my mind, Alfie gave a small shrug. "No, I get it. No choice, right? It sucks that you couldn't get some time off for this, or even just for the day! Even I don't have to do anything more once we leave here."

I hummed. Yeah, I was tired, but I didn't know if I would have wanted to take time off. "I have to live like I'm *not* going to win the *Serves You Right* prize," I explained. Now that there were only three couples left, my odds were much better than they had been at the start.

But Aaron was an amazing cook. He'd been head chef for longer than I'd been in the catering business at all. It would be stupid to assume that I could beat him.

And so, as I'd said, I had to carry on with my work as if I were going to lose. "I need to have that job still available when we finish filming. And I don't want them to think that I've been distracted by all this. I want them to see how good I am, how much I want to keep working for them."

And I did. Obviously, it would be amazing if I could open my own firm and design my own menus. But being ambitious didn't mean I was unhappy where I was.

"I just wish I could skip the bits that aren't actually cooking, at least for one night," I muttered.

Alfie's frown made me want to take it back. Before I could, he was already talking. "Well, can I help?" Alfie asked. "I obviously can't cook anything, but what you're describing is mostly... lifting and carrying things? I can lift and carry things!" The energy he poured into that statement made me laugh. Then, as if to emphasize his point, Alfie flexed his biceps and my breath caught.

Thankfully, he didn't seem to notice. God knew I didn't need even more reason to be embarrassed around him.

"I don't mean to presume, of course, but if it would help you? Unless you don't think I could do it? But you've seen how well I do at following the instructions you give."

And he was right. The reason we worked so well together was that Alfie was brilliant at not only following my instructions but anticipating what might need to happen next.

But would it be weird, the two of us hanging out together outside of filming? The last time we'd spent time alone, I'd almost thrown myself at him. I couldn't afford to let that happen again.

On the other hand, I'd be at work. I wasn't so unprofessional that I'd get distracted from my job by Alfie's mere presence. And there would be other people around.

"It would be a big help," I confirmed. "But... are you sure? Wouldn't you rather hook up with your friends for video games? That sounds like it would be much more fun."

Alfie paused. For a moment it seemed like he might just agree. My stomach sank a little. His offer had been just polite, it was foolish of me to presume it was anything more. But then he shook his head.

"I'd rather help you," Alfie informed me. "The guys and I can play video games any day, it won't make a difference, but helping you might. We make a good team, so just look at it as an extension of that," he suggested before giving me a soft grin.

It made my knees go weak, but I found myself returning the smile. It was impossible not to when Alfie looked so genuinely happy to be able to help me. My heart lifted, soaring up until I felt sure it would fly out of me and into the air between us.

"Okay," I agreed. "Thank you, Alfie. You're such a nice person." I laughed. "I would say that I'd come help you at work if you ever need it, but I don't imagine you'd have much use for someone who barely knows the rules."

Besides, Alfie had a whole team of hockey stars to help him.

"I am such a nice person," Alfie confirmed before giving me a grin. But it was definitely true. I hadn't known Alfie for very long, yet it didn't stop me from feeling like I'd known him for years. There was something very easy to trust about Alfie and part of that was definitely how genuinely nice he was.

It made me feel supported in a way I probably had no right to feel with someone I'd not even known for a whole month. Yet, here we were.

"So?" Alfie asked when I hadn't said anything. "Come on, I'll drive, you clearly need the rest, even if just for the ride there."

I hadn't even thought about the fact that Alfie probably had a car outside! And I couldn't deny that it would be nice to sit back and relax on my way to work for once. My only worry was that it would give me too much time to notice just how good Alfie looked in the seat next to me.

But it didn't end up being as much of a problem as I'd thought it would be. I had to give Alfie directions, and we spent half the journey trying to find a Spotify playlist that both of us were willing to listen to.

My preference was for Spanish music, something with a fast beat and lyrics that I didn't understand and, therefore, wouldn't find distracting. Alfie preferred the music he'd listened to as a teenager, so finding something that catered to us both was a challenge.

It reminded me how different we were, how very incompatible our routines and preferences seemed to be. Maybe that was all for the best, considering how much I felt my heart melting at Alfie's generosity in coming to work with me.

At first, I tried to give him the easy jobs, but he quickly noticed that I was doing more of the heavy-lifting myself than I was letting him do. Another flex of his muscled shoulders reminded me that Alfie was much more built for lifting and carrying than I was, no matter how much yoga I tried to fit in on my days off.

"Okay, okay," I agreed, laughing. "If you really want me to work you hard, you can grab that big box there." The way Alfie lifted it wasn't effortless, but it was nonetheless impressive.

Now that we were away from the cameras, I had more freedom to pick up where we'd left off. Now that I'd had a glimpse into Alfie's childhood, I wanted to know more.

"Where did you and your nana live?" I asked. I had no idea whether Alfie was a Utah native or if this was just where he'd ended up.

"Michigan," Alfie answered easily. "Born and raised. When I got drafted, I moved here. It was weird to live without her and so far away from her, but we managed. About five years it took me to teach her video calling," he laughed, making me smile, too.

There was no way my grandparents would be able to video call; I had tried to teach them. Whatever Alfie was going to say next, he stopped, face darkening a little. Setting the box down, Alfie gave a small shrug.

"My nana died two years ago. She was ill for a little bit before that, but it was still unexpected. That was... tough."

"Oh, Alfie. I'm so sorry." I crossed the distance between us, pulling Alfie into a hug before I had time to question whether it was a smart thing to do.

At first, he stiffened, like he hadn't expected me to touch him. But then his arms wrapped around me in return, giving me a rough squeeze and a gruff 'thanks' against my ear.

Pulling back, I could still feel the lingering heat of his body against mine. "I'm sorry, I didn't mean to bring up bad memories. It's just that, the way you talked about her, I wanted to know more."

"Oh, no," Alfie shook his head. "They're not bad memories. I mean, obviously, her dying is, but... that's just what it is. If I only think about that, then I'm robbing myself of all the nice memories," he pointed out.

That sounded... very mature. Not that Alfie wasn't but I hadn't really expected so much insight. I was lucky, in that grief wasn't something I'd had to deal with yet. My surprise must have shown, because Alfie gave a soft chuckle.

"I've had therapy," he explained. It was striking how confident he sounded, like it was just part of something he needed to do. And obviously, it was, but yeah, I didn't know all that many people openly talking about it. "It's why the team means so much to me," he added. "They're all the family I have left."

That, too, was something I couldn't really imagine. While I wasn't super close to my parents, I had Nadine, two sets of aunts and uncles, and all their other kids, too.

"It sounds like she loved you a lot," I said. "And I'll bet she was proud of you for making it into the Pumas."

Just because hockey wasn't my favorite thing didn't mean I underestimated what an achievement it was to make it to the NHL. "Did she come to see you play?"

"Oh, yes, all the time," Alfie smiled. It was such a sweet smile, like all the memories - the good kind - were floating to the top. "She was great," he nodded. "I think you would have liked her a lot, even if she didn't teach me to eat vegetables," he teased.

My heart fluttered at that, the idea that not only would Alfie's nana like me and I her, but that he might have wanted us to meet. Maybe I was projecting too much onto this conversation. We couldn't do this for so many reasons. And, even if we did, the chances of things working out when we had so little in common...

Biting my lip I returned to the task at hand, finding it easier not to look at Alfie for a moment.

"It's okay," Alfie said. "I don't mind talking about it," he promised and I realized he'd misunderstood my reaction. Maybe that wasn't a bad thing.

"I think that's admirable," I said, and it was totally true. "I wish Didi hadn't made me ask you about it on camera, but you did really well." Obviously, I hadn't known Alfie's nana, but it seemed to me that anyone would've been pleased to hear themselves talked about that way.

As for me, I'd tried to be careful in what I said, not wanting to accidentally hurt my parents' feelings.

"And you were right about me, too," I added. "It was kind of lonely." I didn't blame my parents for that, it was just the downside of having a small family.

Which made me think about how, one day, I wanted a big family of my own, loads of kids running around eating my food. I'd make sure they learned to love vegetables.

But thinking such thoughts was dangerous. Especially with Alfie so close and so helpful.

Luckily for me, more kitchen staff showed up and I found myself directing not just Alfie, but three other burly guys as they carried boxes from the truck to the kitchen.

None of them were as cute as Alfie, but if I kept those thoughts to myself, I could have quite a good time.

Once the other chefs arrived, I told Alfie to go home. We couldn't really use him in the cooking, and besides, he'd already done so much that I felt he deserved a break.

He could still fit in some video gaming with his friends, and I'd see him for our next challenge.

Once he left, I kept thinking about what Alfie had said. He was so open, so genuine, and so unlike anyone else I had ever met. I was sure there were still depths to him that I knew nothing about, and I wanted to spend time finding them out.

Chapter Thirteen

Alfie

It felt unreal to be in the top three of *Serves You Right*. When the competition had first started, I'd been convinced I'd be out in the first week. Then, after meeting Maya, I had hoped that wouldn't be the case, for her sake. But the truth was, despite not wanting to let Maya down, I still hadn't expected us to do this well.

Maya definitely deserved it, though. She worked so hard and she loved it. Watching her cook had quickly become one of my favorite parts about *Serves You Right*. And so had helping out. I hadn't expected to actually be in any way useful in this show, but Maya made me feel like I could be.

Every next task felt like so much more pressure, though.

If at first I'd thought we'd fail on week one, now it was getting closer and closer to the end and, well, my competitive side was kicking in a lot more. It was us, Maxine and her chef Karl, and James and Aaron left. There was no way that I wanted arrogant James and equally arrogant Aaron to win.

Maya was much nicer about her opinions but I knew she mostly agreed. She might admire Aaron and his achievements, but that didn't mean that she still didn't want to beat him.

So when we showed up for our week five challenge, I was ready to fight. Metaphorically, of course. So far, I'd just done my best without really pushing myself, but if we were going to win, I needed to do more.

"Whatever it is this week, we've got to smash it," I informed Maya seriously. "Next week is the finale and we can do this. Let's kick James and Aaron out and then we can just hang with Maxine."

Maya laughed, tying her apron behind her as the camera crews set up all around us. "Don't make me more nervous than I already am," she warned. But Maya didn't look nervous. She looked excited, and I knew it was the prospect of facing another challenge, putting together another unexpected meal.

It seemed to take far longer than usual for Didi to position everyone the way she wanted. I wondered what was going on, why they needed so many different angles. I hoped they weren't going to ask to cook something huge, like a tower of cake or anything.

Finally, Alix stepped up to her mark and beamed at us all. "We've got a little help for today's challenge," she announced. "A group of very hungry young men who will be familiar to at least one of you..."

From her left, I heard a very recognizable cheer, and then the Pumas began running into shot, lining up behind Alix.

Chuck, who was last, detoured to give me an aggressively friendly thump on the back, draping my Pumas' shirt over one shoulder.

"Alfie," Alix asked, "would you care to explain who's here?"

I blinked at Alix and then at the rest of my team. "Um, some assholes?" I answered and Didi told me off before I'd even finished the word. The guys laughed, though. "They're my team, Alix," I said, knowing that they could just edit out the bit where I'd sworn.

"Though, I don't know why they're here?" I added truthfully. No one had mentioned this to me, neither the producers on the show nor any of the guys, which was more shocking. Normally, they couldn't keep a secret to save their lives.

I could see the smug, pleased-with-themselves grins plastered on every face. It looked like the whole team was here! It was hard to imagine how they'd kept that to themselves.

"That part I can explain," Alix said. "They're your judges today. You have to put together a meal that not only fills up their appetites, but also fulfills their nutritional requirements."

She turned to Luke, who'd stepped forward a little. "Can you explain a bit about what those are?"

I hardly had to listen; I knew exactly what their nutritional requirements were, because they were exactly the same as mine. Luke talked about needing lots of energy the day of a big game, but nothing too heavy that would make players feel sluggish or sleepy.

A grin was stealing across my face. This was going to be easy. How could I possibly lose a challenge that was all about hockey?

"All your food will be served up anonymously, so the Pumas won't know who cooked what dish. Whoever gets the highest score will be our winner, and whoever scores the lowest will be going home."

Maya shifted next to me, biting her lower lip. "I hope you know what everyone likes, Alfie," she muttered to me.

"Ah yes, because we're going to cook twenty plus different dishes?" I frowned. There was absolutely no way to specifically cook something for everyone on the team. But that also wasn't actually what we were being asked to do. "Sorry," I muttered, shooting Maya an apologetic look, realizing that my comment must have been pretty snappy. "I just want to win."

And I wanted to win for *her*.

Alix went on to explain how we were to prepare three separate dishes. We would also be given a list of all the things Luke was allergic to, so at least one of the dishes had to exclude all of those so he, too, could eat it.

The guys gave me grins and fistbumps on their way out, in no way making this look biased.

Turning to Maya, I gave a small sigh. "Luke is allergic to like everything," I informed her. "This is going to be so hard." But it was the challenge before the finale, right? So it probably had to be hard.

Maya nodded, almost as if she had heard my thought and was agreeing with it. "I was really starting to get a sense of what the judges liked and didn't like," she added. "But now that we've got a whole different set of judges, I feel a little lost."

She shrugged one shoulder, glancing up at me through her bangs. "At least I'm used to cooking big portions for a lot of people. That should help somewhat." It had helped us before, in the canapés challenge, so I nodded.

"We probably can't do pizza again," Maya noted, frowning. "What else do guys like?"

The question made me laugh, the way Maya had phrased it almost as if guys - and specifically hockey players - were an unknown species.

"Most of them like vegetables," I teased.

A lot of the guys were foodies, I knew as much because I got shit for not being a foodie. "Steak is always popular." Whenever we had to agree on somewhere most people wanted to go it was steak. "Chicken, too. We all eat a lot of chicken, so if we could make something different with chicken, I bet they'd be excited."

I knew I would be, so it was a good shout.

I could practically see the wheels turning in Maya's brain. She lit up with an inner glow that took my breath away, despite the fact I'd seen it four times before. Her passion for food - and for coming up with ideas about food - was still impressive.

"Something different," she mused, not quite looking at me. She'd retreated to an inner world, probably remembering the recipes in all those cookbooks that I'd seen on the shelves of her kitchen.

Reaching for a notepad, Maya jotted down a couple of different words, then glanced back at me. "There's a blueberry-mustard sauce that I made for Nadine. It might go with chicken or steak. And we could do a salad alongside it - or something more carb-loaded?"

Blueberry-mustard sauce sounded absolutely insane but maybe insane was what we needed to win this. It definitely didn't seem like a thing that many of the guys would've ever had before, even the ones who were really into their food.

"Okay," I drew out slowly. "We'll do a blueberry-mustard sauce. Salad is fine but maybe... kind of boring?" It wasn't ever going to be my preferred choice, anyway, but that didn't mean much. "Maybe it'd be cool if we could make three dishes that all go together? Like, ah, puzzle pieces?"

Maya crossed out where she'd written salad, then lifted the pen to tap against her lower lip. "So maybe something potato-based, to go with the steak?" she suggested. "Not fries, because everyone will have had those before. Maybe potatoes boulangere or tartiflette?"

She only needed one glance at my face to know I had no idea what either of those were. "It's sort of like a potato casserole," she explained. "I bet I could put mustard in the sauce, and that would tie it to the steak even more."

I nodded. I couldn't quite imagine what Maya meant, but I trusted her that it would be delicious. And it sounded more exciting than salad.

"And then what about a third dish?" she asked. "Another side, but one that Luke can eat?" she suggested.

"Well, it sounds like mustard is going in everything," I pointed out. "So we want to do something with that. Are the chicken and steak our mains? With the sauce and the potato?" I felt a bit like I was trying to catch up with Maya and her ideas. They sounded good, sure, but I wasn't feeling like I was contributing very much.

I tried hard to think of what I knew Luke would like. He did like steak, it was easy and almost always guaranteed not to trigger one of his many allergic reactions. Looking at the list we'd been provided of everything Luke was allergic to, I gave a small hum.

"Could we do a desert?" I asked, remembering how excited Luke got about the cream puffs El sometimes made him. "Luke's rarely allowed any of the deserts, I mean none of us are, but Luke and his allergies especially."

Maya came closer, her arm brushing against mine as she also looked down at the list. "Well, Luke won't be able to eat the potato, unless I find something I can use as a replacement for cream, so maybe he needs a dessert to make up for that."

She tapped the pen against the paper now, making the words 'eggs', 'soy' and 'dairy' dance a little in the bright lights.

"We could make a cashew and coconut cheesecake?" she suggested after a moment. "That's not really linked to anything else, so would it still count as a puzzle piece?"

"Maybe if we made a blueberry sauce for the cake, too? Obviously not with mustard in it, but you can have a blueberry sauce for a cake, right?" It made more sense to me than blueberry sauce for a meat dish, so why not.

I found myself quite distracted by how close Maya was. Her perfume was so soft, barely noticeable at all, but with how close she stood, I could smell it. I wanted to reach out, to brush my hand over hers. Heat shot through me, a sudden desire that made me take a step back before I did something stupid.

"Yeah, we can do that," Maya confirmed, apparently oblivious to both my arousal and my awkwardness. "So then we've got blueberry in one dish, mustard in another, and the main course in the middle brings them both together." She looked up, bright-eyed and beaming. "I see what you mean about puzzle pieces now!"

It felt so good to have her understand me that I almost closed the distance between us. I would've loved to wrap my arms around Maya, pull her close and let her feel the sparks that exploded through me just from knowing we were on the same wavelength.

But giving in would mean disqualification, and I couldn't allow that. We had to beat Aaron and James.

"Do you think that sounds like enough food?" Maya asked. "We don't want them to still be hungry."

"I think so," I hummed, glad that we could talk about the food as a distraction. It made me realize just how different that was from how I thought even a few weeks back. Food had never been something I wanted to talk about, but now, with Maya? Well, it was impossible not to enjoy it, not when her face lit up so much even at the mention of it.

We set to work, which also worked well as a distraction. Maya told me what to do, what bowls to get, what to mix together. We fell into silence, working together well. The cameras moved away from us then, our actual cooking not that interesting.

When Alix announced we only had five minutes left, I glanced at Maya and then at all the food we've set out. "I think we've got this," I decided. But I could also tell that both James and Maxine's food looked great.

"I imagine you're against sabotage?" I whispered jokingly to Maya. She was definitely too nice for sabotage. Even I was too nice for sabotage.

Her eyes widened for a moment before she realized I was joking. "No, Alfie, that wouldn't be right." She objected. "If we win, I want to win because I made the best food, not because somebody else messed up."

And, well, I could understand that. I felt similarly about hockey, wanting to win on my own merits, or the team's.

"I'm glad it's anonymous," Maya added. "I even made some grilled green vegetables so they wouldn't be able to guess which was yours by the lack of them."

That made me laugh, but it was pretty good thinking on Maya's part. Besides, the rest of the team didn't have my problem with eating anything green, so they'd probably appreciate it.

"What do we do while we wait?" Karl asked from beside me as the crew carried the last of the plates away to wherever the Pumas were doing their tasting.

"Stand around nervously?" Maxine suggested and we all chuckled; she wasn't wrong.

It was weird to think that mine and Maya's fate was in the hands of my friends. I had to hope that Maya and I had done enough to wow them. I felt that we had, but we were up against strong competition.

After they'd filmed us standing around nervously, Didi stepped up. "We're going to shoot some interviews while we wait," she informed us. "Just reflections about how far you guys have come, what your relationship is like with your partner." I could swear that when she said it, Didi looked right at me.

"Since it's your team who are here today, we'll start with you," she explained, beckoning me back to the seating area with the backdrop of cooking implements. Maya and I had been interviewed there once before, and I remembered how nervous she'd been.

This time, it was my turn to attempt to swallow down the apprehension.

"So, Alfie, did you get to contribute a lot of input to today's challenge?" Didi asked, once the camera person had given us the green light to go ahead with the interview.

I blinked at the camera and then at Didi, before nodding. "Yeah," I answered but it wasn't enough; Didi told me to answer in full, so when they came to edit it, everything made sense. "Sorry."

"Um, yes. I feel like I got to contribute a fair bit today. Maya is always very good at allowing me to feel included, even if I'm definitely the one who knows the least about cooking." I didn't specify that it was out of the two of us, because that wasn't even true. It was out of everyone on the show.

"And you enjoy working with Maya?"

"Yes, of course," I nodded.

"Full answers, Alfie," Didi reminded.

"Right. Yeah, I really like working with Maya. She's a great chef but she also takes the time to find out what I might like and listens to my input. Maya makes me feel involved, like we're a team."

Didi raised her eyebrows and stared at me so hard that I had to concentrate on not squirming in my seat.

"A team that you'd like to continue after the competition?" she asked. "Fans have noticed that the two of you seem very close. They've even come up with a couple name for you, I'm sure you've heard."

And yes, of course, I had, but I had to tread carefully in answering this kind of question. I couldn't say anything that might make Didi suspect there was more going on than there actually was.

Not that there was anything going on.

Maya and I hadn't done anything that went against our contracts. This competition mattered to Maya and therefore it mattered to me, too. It wasn't what I had expected but it was true.

"Sure, Maya's great," I shrugged. "But we're just partners on a cooking show, right? I know that people like to think there's more between us, but there really isn't. #Alfaya is cute and all, but it's not accurate to reality." None of that was actually a lie.

What came next, though, was more of one. But I felt like I had to say something, especially after how close Maya had stood to me today, how much I'd wanted to just reach out and touch her.

"I'm actually already seeing someone," I told Didi. "So, yeah."

If I'd expected that to stop the questions, I'd made a big mistake. Didi practically lit up, sitting up straighter so that she looked weirdly tall in her little plastic seat.

"Ooh, is this a *Serves You Right* exclusive, Alfie? I didn't know you were in a relationship already."

I could feel my pulse race. Shit. Was I going to have to make up details about an imaginary girlfriend?

But I was saved by the bell. Or rather, by the deafening cheer of half a dozen Pumas.

"Alfie!" Chuck raced over to me, throwing an arm over my shoulders. "Man, that food was so delicious. Chase practically couldn't believe that you'd made any of it." I must have frowned, because Chuck shook his head energetically. "Levi said of course you did, and Maya, too. We all put bets on which dishes we think are yours."

"And what would this competition be if you weren't betting on me," I laughed. Looking over at Didi, I shrugged. "Are we done? I assume the results will be announced soon?" And really, if we could be done with this interview before I had to lie about stuff, that'd be awesome.

Didi frowned but from how excited the Pumas were, she must have realized she was hardly going to contain them. "Yeah, we can be done," Didi nodded. "Thanks, Alfie."

"So which foods did you like the most?" I asked but before Chuck could answer, Didi stepped in.

"No, no. Don't ruin it. We want to catch the reactions on camera! So just wait a little bit."

Chuck looked as if he were about to tell me his favorite anyway, but Levi elbowed him in the ribs. It made me laugh how seriously Levi was taking this, but Didi clearly appreciated it because she gave him a huge smile as she shepherded us back to the main filming area.

I walked beside Chuck, the two of us hanging back from the crowd a little. "Seriously, Alfie, I hope we haven't accidentally sent you home," he said. "That would really suck if it was our fault you and Maya got eliminated."

It would suck.

But I still had faith in what we'd cooked.

"Obviously, if that happens, it'll be whoever bet on me going home this week," I joked. It helped me to squish my nerves down. Leaving now would suck, this meant so much to Maya.

But Chuck was probably right in that having my own team be the reason I lost the competition would be worse.

I just had to hope that they loved what Maya and I had come up with.

Chapter Fourteen
Maya

My heart was in my throat the whole time Didi was interviewing Alfie. His competitive spirit had transferred itself to me, especially when it came to Aaron and James. I wanted to win, not only for the grand prize, but because I wanted to show that my understanding of flavors and my ideas about food were good enough to challenge the best chefs in the city.

I just hoped that they were. When the Pumas surged towards us, dragging Alfie along in their wake, I felt sure we'd find out whether our gamble had been a success.

But Didi got in the way, insisting that she wanted to film everybody's first reactions. Luckily for me, the cameras were already set up, so we didn't have to wait too long.

Everybody loved the steak, just as Alfie had suggested. But it was the unexpected combination of blueberry and mustard that seemed to have put us over the edge.

I practically danced on the spot, only just catching myself before I could reach for Alfie's hand and give it a victorious squeeze.

The challenge didn't have an official winner - apparently, that would have sucked the suspense out of next week's final - but it was pretty clear from what the Pumas said that they'd enjoyed our meal at least as much as anything else that had been presented.

Of course, no matter how good all the food was at this stage in the competition, one couple still had to go. Alix didn't make us wait too long before she announced that it was Maxine and Karl who'd cooked the lowest-scoring dish.

I hadn't made friends with them as much as Alfie had, but I was still sad to see them so disappointed. And I knew Alfie would feel both bad on their behalf and also crestfallen that we still hadn't beaten Aaron and James.

In a way, I wasn't too surprised. Aaron had always seemed like the strongest chef in the competition. And if James wasn't as helpful as Alfie was, Aaron was clearly good enough to make up for it. It made sense that he'd be one of the finalists.

What shocked me was that I was the other one! The euphoria and disbelief seemed to steal over me slowly. By the time I'd fully realized just how glad I was, Alfie had already been swept off by his friends.

That took the wind out of my sails a little. It felt weird to go home without even a word of celebration.

When I got back to my apartment, I realized *why* the Pumas had been so insistent on taking Alfie right after filming had finished: they had a game that night. Nadine was already installed on our sofa, with veggie sticks and the leftover dip that I'd made a few nights before.

Feeling lost, I sank onto the seat beside her. "Can I watch with you?" I asked. After everything Alfie had said about hockey, I wanted to learn to enjoy it. It was so important to him, and Alfie had made such an effort to support me in my work that it was only fair I do the same.

Maybe watching on the TV instead of in person would make the violence a little more bearable.

Nadine didn't bother hiding her surprise and I gave a small shrug. "Yeah, sure, sure," she agreed before getting up and walking to the kitchen. When she returned, Nadine was carrying two beers. "We have to do it the right way," she informed me with a grin.

"So, obviously, we're supporting the Pumas. They're playing in blue," she added and I rolled my eyes. Even I knew what color the Pumas played in. "How was filming today?"

That made me smile, still relishing the fact that we had made it through to the final. And doubtless, Nadine could tell just from my expression that we hadn't been eliminated.

"It was different," I answered honestly. "We weren't allowed to be in the room when the judges were trying our food." I wanted to watch the Pumas reactions, which would be the first time I'd tuned in to *Serves You Right* to see something that I hadn't already witnessed in person.

Trying to keep the smirk off my face, I added, "You'll like this episode. We should watch it together!"

"Oh, yes? You'll actually watch it with me? We should definitely do that." Nadine nodded excitedly. It was true that, since the comments about #alfaya, I hadn't bothered watching the show, worried that I'd hate how I looked or sounded. But also, I wasn't sure how I'd feel about seeing Alfie and me together on screen.

From the following we'd gathered on social media, I knew that we were popular, but it felt a little scary to see why.

Biting my lip, I wondered if I should ask Nadine about it. Unlike me, she did watch the show. "What?" Nadine asked, basically reading my mind. It was the curse of being so close to my cousin, I supposed.

"Does it really look like I've got a huge crush on Alfie?" I asked. "I mean, I saw those first tweets about #alfaya, but has it gotten any better?" Alfie had made a deliberate effort not to look like we were closer than we ought to be, I knew that. What I didn't know was whether it had *worked*.

It was hard for me to judge. My own feelings kept getting in the way. Memories of that night at Luke's party, of Alfie sitting in my kitchen sipping coffee when I'd felt sure that there was something more brewing between us.

But since then, he'd kept his distance and so had I. It was the right thing to do, but it only made me more aware of his body when we were together.

Nadine seemed to think about my question before she shook her head. "Not really. I mean, it doesn't look like you have more of a crush on him than he does on you," she teased, making me blush. "I think the whole social media stuff, it's just that you both look... cute. I'm sure a lot of it is just editing."

Except I wasn't as convinced.

"Unless... it's not? Do you have a crush on Alfie, Maya? You can tell me," Nadine said, bumping her shoulder against mine. "Do you like the hot, hot NHL player?" she teased.

My blush turned positively scarlet. But I couldn't deny that Alfie was just as hot as Nadine said. And, really, it would be a relief to have somebody to talk to about the feelings I felt sure were bubbling under the surface.

For me, at least. I carried a lot more doubt about Alfie's feelings. Sure, he'd been attracted to me that night in the kitchen, but that didn't necessarily mean that he wanted to act on it.

After all, he must get women throwing themselves at him all the time. Why would he want to be with me when he could find himself a real hockey fan who understood his passion so much better than I ever could?

"I think it might be more than a crush," I admitted. "I'm not obsessed with him or anything, but..." How could I put it into words? "I just feel so much more relaxed when he's around. And I want to know everything about him, but I don't want to pressure him by asking too many questions when we're on camera!"

Nadine turned towards me, distracted from the game by my revelation. "I wish we could spend time together without all the pressure of the competition, you know? But I'm afraid that if we did, something might happen."

"But there's only one week left?" Nadine pointed out. "Surely, then... you are free to do whatever, right?" Except it wasn't as easy as all that, because there was still publicity to do. But after that... well, that was scary, too. Without any restrictions, would Alfie and I even find each other interesting?

I didn't think that for me it was that we weren't allowed to, but maybe both of us were a little affected by that. And then there was the fact that we didn't have all that much in common. Alfie didn't like food and I didn't like hockey.

It just all felt a bit impossible.

"What if Alfie doesn't want to do whatever?" I asked. "Or what if he wants just a physical thing?" That had never been my style, and no matter how hot Alfie was, I didn't think I wanted to start now.

I wanted to get to know Alfie, to be allowed to be there for all the stuff that went beyond just physical chemistry. "I have no idea if he's even interested in me that way."

Sure, Alfie was supportive and enthusiastic around me, but he seemed to be that way around everyone.

"I just don't want to get my hopes up if it's not going to come to anything."

Nadine looked a little skeptical. "I think maybe you should watch the show," she told me. "If you saw how Alfie looks at you... well, I suppose he looks at you kind of the same way you look at him."

I wasn't quite sure what to make of that information. Was it true? Did Alfie... it just seemed like reading too much into nothing. Yes, we got on. Yes, I enjoyed spending time with Alfie. But we saw each other once a week for a few hours filming. That didn't mean we'd be able to make things work past that.

Not to mention that we had no way of finding out with the filming still going on.

But there was only a week left, as Nadine had pointed out. Could I?

"Surely, you've got to take some risks sometimes, Maya."

That brought me up short. Nadine knew me too well - well enough that her words were painfully true. I wasn't a risk-taker. The lack of any serious relationship in my life could definitely be put down to how safely I played everything. That and the fact most of my energy went into my work.

But here was Alfie, already a part of my work, not to mention the sweetest and most genuine guy I'd ever met. Maybe Nadine was right. If I didn't take a risk, I might regret it for the rest of my life.

"Well, it still has to wait until we've finished filming," I pointed out. "But maybe you should talk me through the rest of this hockey match. Then I can impress him with how much I've learned!"

It was a task Nadine was only too happy to take on. I still winced whenever the Pumas got slammed into the sides of the rink, but I pushed myself to keep watching. And it did help a little to see them push right back. This definitely wasn't one-sided aggression.

By the time the game was over, I'd picked up a few terms that I thought I could use in conversation. And I felt that my determination to see past my initial prejudices against the sport was a good first step in my campaign to actually take a risk.

While Nadine got herself ready to sleep, I texted Alfie to congratulate him and the rest of the team on their win. He didn't reply at once, but I knew he had the press to deal with, not to mention celebrating with the rest of the Pumas.

I decided to have an early night, hoping that Alfie would send me a nice message to wake up to the next morning.

~*~

A few days later, when Nadine and I sat down to watch the latest episode of *Serves You Right*, there were definite butterflies in my stomach. This would be the deciding factor for me. If Alfie really looked at me as if he liked me in more than a physical way, I was going to take a risk and ask him out.

Not until our last day of filming, of course. I still didn't want to get disqualified. But there was only one more week and, if we didn't win, then they couldn't do anything to me after the final even if we were still contracted to do publicity.

As I'd predicted, Nadine was wild with excitement when the Pumas ran onto the screen.

"I don't know how you can be jealous that I got to cook for them when you've already spent the night with one of them!" I teased.

Nadine snorted, giving a small dismissive wave. I hadn't heard a lot about her night with Chuck, but I did know that they'd not bothered with anything more than one night. It definitely wasn't something I would have wanted, but Nadine seemed perfectly happy with how that had turned out.

Reaching for the bowl of popcorn she'd insisted we make for this, Nadine shrugged. "There's still a whole team I haven't had," she informed me, the joke making my eyes widen and cheeks redden. Nadine laughed when she noticed.

"I'm only joking," she promised. "I'm not going to bang the whole team. Anyway, I think loads of them are in a relationship already."

That came as news to me. Alfie hadn't talked much about the rest of his team and their romantic relationships. Maybe he hadn't thought it was relevant. Or maybe he hadn't wanted to give me the impression that hockey players were looking for somebody to settle down with.

It was so easy to second guess myself. I could make almost anything into a sign that Alfie didn't want to be with me. But weren't there just as many signs that he did?

I watched carefully as we traded ideas back and forth, our heads bent far closer together than I'd realized at the time.

"I do think we work well together," I said. "For someone who doesn't eat a lot of ingredients, Alfie's very good at coming up with ideas about food."

"Probably had to be versatile as a kid, since he and his grandmother didn't have a lot of money," Nadine pointed out. That felt like it had come out of nowhere. When she turned to look at me, Nadine snorted. "I watch the show," she reminded me.

Oh, right.

Somehow, the fact that *everyone* had seen the conversation we'd had about Alfie growing up had escaped from my mind. In fact, most of our conversations had been witnessed by whoever watched the show. That was a lot of people. It felt the intimacy being drained from the connection I thought Alfie and I shared.

"Anyway," Nadine said as she shrugged, turning back to the TV. "I'm excited to see them enjoy your food. Obviously, I know you didn't get booted out, otherwise you'd be crying and we'd need more ice cream in the freezer."

I laughed; I really couldn't deny it. Nadine and I had realized pretty quickly that she was always going to know whether or not I'd been eliminated. As long as she didn't tell anyone, I didn't really think of it as being against the rules that I'd agreed to.

After a commercial break, we watched Maxine and Karl putting their meal together. They weren't struggling, but knowing that they scored the lowest, I could kind of see why. Their food looked yummy, but there was nothing particularly original about it. The Pumas could probably get the same meal in any decent restaurant in Salt Lake City.

Before we could watch the Pumas tuck into their meal, the footage cut to something else I hadn't seen before. Alfie sat, alone, in front of the interview background and I realized this must've been footage of the questions Didi had asked while I'd been waiting to find out what the Pumas thought of our blueberry and mustard puzzle pieces.

"I really like working with Maya," the Alfie on my screen announced. "She's a great chef but she also takes the time to find out what I might like and listens to my input."

I blushed, glancing sideways at Nadine to see what she made of this declaration.

"See!" she nodded. "He thinks you make a great team." And I couldn't deny the fact that it felt good to hear Alfie say these things. It was easy to be on Alfie's team, I hardly felt like I needed to try. Yet, when I did, that came easily as well. It made our relationship feel good and like it had so much potential.

Then all of that kind of crumbled as I heard what Alfie said next.

"But we're just partners at a cooking show, right?" Alfie on the screen told the camera, making my heart sink. "I know that people like to think there's more between us, but there really isn't. #Alfaya is cute and all, but it's not accurate to reality."

Cute and all, but not accurate to reality.

The words felt like they cut right into my heart, breath suddenly catching in my throat.

"Oh," Nadine breathed, her head snapping to me. "Maya," she drew out softly but Alfie wasn't even done.

"I'm actually already seeing someone. So, yeah," Alfie said just before the interview cut, a voiceover announcing that we were learning it here first, an exclusive from Alfie. An exclusive about dating someone who definitely wasn't me.

Cold swept over me, from the crown of my head to the tips of my toes, leaving me a frozen statue next to Nadine. For a moment, I couldn't even breathe. Seeing someone. How could Alfie be seeing someone? He'd never mentioned a girlfriend.

And did that mean I'd been imagining the chemistry between us the night he drove me home?

My internal temperature flipped a switch, shame burning through me.

"Oh, my God," I murmured. My hands lifted almost on their own, covering my face and creating a wall between me and the world.

I couldn't believe how much of an idiot I'd been. "I was really starting to think he liked me."

When Nadine didn't say anything straight away, I knew she didn't know what to say. In general, Nadine was pretty great at not lacking words. When she did finally speak, it was almost worse, because I could hear the pity in her tone.

"Maybe..." she started but I turned to give her a look. Making excuses or trying to think of ways this could still be okay wasn't actually going to help me. Watching tonight's episode of *Serves You Right* was meant to be the deciding factor in whether Alfie and I could make this work.

It hadn't turned out the way I had hoped.

But a decision was clearly reached.

Chapter Fifteen

Alfie

For days after the Pumas had visited the *Serves You Right* set to be involved with the challenge, all the talk at training was about how much fun they'd had, how cool it had been. There had also, obviously, been a lot of chirping about how surprised they were that the food had been so tasty despite me being part of the team that cooked it.

Mostly, though, everyone was excited about me and Maya having made it to the final. It was impossible at this point not to hope that we might win. Yes, James and Aaron were going to be tough competition, but Maya and I... we had something special.

Of course, then the episode aired and the chirping turned from how surprised everyone was about me being able to make something edible to how I'd made up a girlfriend.

"Why would you even say that?" Chuck had laughed, but the honest truth was, it made sure that no one on the show would see more than there was between Maya and me.

I didn't tell that to the guys. I was sure they wouldn't get it.

It was easy enough to dismiss, to say that it had just been something the producers had wanted me to say. There was no way I could lie to the guys when they basically knew everywhere I went and everyone I saw. And besides them and Maya (and the people on the show), I hardly saw anyone at all.

But this way, things would be easier.

Or well, so I had assumed before the internet exploded. Apparently, the fans of #alfaya were broken-hearted. It was still kind of weird to me that so many people cared about this.

With the finale fast approaching, I tried to squish my nerves. Having played plenty of games competitively, I was sure we could do this. But it did occur to me that what helped me feel confident about hockey was the fact that I got to practice.

That wasn't something that Maya and I had done, but maybe since this was it, this was the final stretch, we should.

I texted Maya asking if she felt it'd be useful to do that. Maybe go through some ingredients, practice some simple stuff I could do to help. Obviously, we had no idea what the finale would be but some practice wouldn't hurt.

It wasn't until I was waiting for Maya to get there that I realized that maybe I felt a bit nervous about this, too. Maya had never been to my place before, but it made more sense for us to practice cooking here. My kitchen was bigger, albeit almost definitely not as well equipped.

"I do own stuff," I promised Maya as I led her through to the kitchen. "Like bowls and knives and... food." I'd even especially gone out and bought a bunch of vegetables that I had no idea what to do with.

She paused in the doorway, looking around the room with slightly glazed eyes. Even though my house was pretty normal-sized, my kitchen was still a lot bigger than what Maya had in her apartment.

"It's... very clean," she said, making me frown. It wasn't that her remark wasn't true - the whole house was pretty clean - but it almost sounded like it should have had a teasing tone to it that just hadn't been there.

Coming to stand at one of the counters, Maya rested her hands lightly on the surface. "I don't really know what you want us to do," she admitted. "I guess it might be helpful if I could tell you to handle the cooking of one or two elements so that I can focus on more complicated things. But where do we start?"

"Well," I started because I had actually thought about this. "You could teach me to chop things?" When Maya gave me a look, I rushed in to add. "No, hear me out. I do okay, I know, but I've seen how you cut things and it's so much..." Well, I was about to say it was so much cooler, which it was, but that wasn't the point. "Faster."

Maya, in general, worked a lot faster than me, so I figured that if I could be even half as quick, we'd save a lot of time. The finale would involve big quantities of food, that was the whole premise of *Serves You Right*, so we did know that.

Maya looked uncertain. At least, that was my impression. There was none of her usual sparkle about her; she seemed almost uninterested, even though I knew how important the competition was to her.

It made me wonder if maybe she was coming down with something. I hoped not. It seemed unlikely that they would reschedule filming, and I needed Maya at her best.

"Okay, I can try," she agreed, reaching into her bag for what I now recognized was a set of chef's knives in a travel wrap.

She rolled out the fabric, explaining each knife to me and showing me how to hold the vegetable in place with my knuckles so that I wouldn't risk chopping off a finger.

Just as I thought I was getting the hang of it, Maya blurted out something that completely distracted my attention.

"Were you going to tell me that you had a girlfriend?"

"What?" I frowned before it struck me.

Right, of course. Maya had seen the episode, she'd seen the interview in which I had said I was seeing someone. Now was the time to come clean. To tell Maya that I'd only said it to throw any suspicions off us. But there wasn't an us.

All of my thoughts about how, if there was an us, I risked breaking Maya's heart rushed through me. We had so little in common. Even now, the way she'd looked around my kitchen, it reminded me how much Maya loved food.

Why would she date someone like me? I didn't even know the name of half of the things we were cutting up right now.

"It's, ah, new," I lied, feeling my stomach drop.

The shock on Maya's face was unmistakable. It was enough to make me wish I could call the words back and tell her the truth. But how would I explain that? It was bad enough that we had nothing in common, it would be much worse to tell Maya that I didn't want to date her because I didn't think it would last.

It was better this way, letting her believe that I'd met someone else.

At least, I was almost sure that it was.

"Oh." Her voice was so small. I could barely hear her over the sound of her knife hitting the chopping block over and over again, obliterating the vegetable into smaller and smaller chunks.

She shook her head, her lips lifting in the ghost of a smile. Almost as if she knew she was supposed to pretend to be happy for me, but couldn't quite manage it. Or maybe I was imagining things.

"I'm sorry," she said after a moment. "After all, there's no reason you should tell me first. It's not as if we're friends, really."

That shouldn't have hurt as much as it did.

Over the weeks I'd known Maya, without really thinking about it, she'd very much become my friend. It was different from the guys on the team. They were my family, while Maya was... I wasn't even sure what. Certainly a friend.

But if she was my friend, I wouldn't be lying to her right now, right?

"I would have told you," I decided. "Just, you know, the timing wasn't right."

"Sure." Maya's agreement sounded hollow to my ears. I hated the thought that I might lose her over this - but then remembered that she hadn't even been mine to begin with.

She shrugged one shoulder. "With the show and everything, I imagine it's been pretty hectic."

What struck me was that it really hadn't been. I'd enjoyed being on the show, and getting to hang out with Maya as we filmed our challenges. I only hoped this wouldn't be the end of that.

"That's really all the technique there is to chopping things," Maya said, drawing my attention back to the knife skills I was supposed to be learning. "After that, it's just practice to get faster."

"Right." I nodded.

The silence between us stretched, making things feel more and more awkward. I wanted to apologize, to say that this was all a lie. To fix things in any way I could. But that wasn't an option.

Even if I admitted that there was no one else, that didn't mean there could be something between me and Maya. Besides, she'd been the one to say that we weren't even friends.

"So... I guess I'll just practice more? Do you... is there other stuff you want to show me?" If I'd known how awkward this would get, I wouldn't have invited Maya over. And that thought hurt, too.

Unlike her, I had thought of Maya as my friend.

"I should probably show you something else." Maya didn't sound enthusiastic about it. Suddenly, an afternoon in my kitchen with her was the last thing I wanted. But I'd been the one to invite her here, and I could hardly send her away again so soon.

Besides, even if she didn't think of me as a friend, we would still have to work together if we wanted to win the competition.

So Maya showed me how to make a basic sauce, explaining that from that she could add whatever she wanted for flavor.

I doubted I'd remember all the steps, but at least I'd have some idea what Maya was talking about if she reminded me of them.

"I'm not sure there's much else we can usefully do," she said at last. It felt like a relief.

Doing my best not to actually show that, I helped Maya put her knives away. I had thought about asking Maya to have dinner with me, maybe order a takeaway but now I was glad that offer hadn't come before this awkward conversation.

Instead, I walked her out. We had a few days before the finale, so I promised to practice my chopping skills. If Maya cared, she did a great job at now showing it.

When the door closed behind her, I let out a sigh.

This had gone absolutely disastrously and it was all my fault.

Somehow, in trying not to hurt Maya, I'd done exactly that.

~*~

Even without talking to Maya in the days after our awkward exchange, I still felt bad. The emotions were hard to untangle. I knew that I had no right to feel upset. If anything, Maya should be upset with me.

And she was.

Or at least, that was very much what it had felt like.

I had no solutions. I'd lied to her and it wasn't something I knew how to go back on. Nor did I think that I should. There was a reason for the things that Maya thought of me. We couldn't do this.

Yet, despite knowing that, the thoughts of Maya didn't seem to want to leave my head. In the end, I decided that I had to talk to someone about it. The guys were the obvious first choice, but even without talking to them, it was pretty easy to predict what the advice would be.

So, I decided to go a different route.

"Hey, Didi, you got a moment?" I asked on the day before the finale was being filmed. I'd gotten to the studio hours before, nerves twisting in my stomach more than they ever did before a hockey match.

Didi blinked at me behind her glasses, but it only took her a moment to reach a decision. "Of course I have time for you, Alfie," she assured. "I hope you're not here to say that you can't film with us today?"

She ushered me inside, finding a place where we could both sit and talk.

"What's up? Pre-finale nerves?" she asked me.

"A bit," I admitted, because that wasn't actually untrue. "It's kind of weird, I'm not used to being nervous. But I'm a lot more confident in my hockey skills." Not that this was why I was here. It was easier, though, to talk about this, to distract myself from the real reason I had come to speak to Didi.

I worried that she might not actually be able to help me. Did she have a responsibility to report my relationship with Maya? But we didn't actually have a relationship. In fact, Maya had said that we weren't even friends.

"You know those questions you asked me at the interview last week? About Maya and me? Can I ask why?"

"Oh." She paused, frowned, tilted her head slightly to one side. "Well, to put it bluntly, Alfie, because that's what the viewers are interested in. Not only in that, of course, but they seem to have latched on to the idea of the two of you."

That much I knew just from existing on Twitter. It had somewhat died down after my announcements that I was seeing someone else, but not entirely.

"You work well together, that's obvious, and that's also appealing to people. Since they can't actually taste the food you guys make, they can't judge their favorite on that. They judge it on personality, and you and Maya both have appealing personalities."

Those were the answers I had expected. She'd asked because it was good TV. Which was... fine. Kind of. "What if I had said that there was something between Maya and I?" Surely, that would have made it something that the fans wanted to hear, but it would also break the rules.

"The contract we signed, it says we'd get disqualified if... you know," I pointed out. "Not that we are," I rushed in to add. Today was the last day, plus the publicity after, and then, in a few weeks, Maya and I would be free of the contracts.

And we'd do nothing about it, because we weren't even friends.

"The audience don't know that," Didi pointed out. "To them, it seems like a nice story, like a modern Cinderella. Maya meets this handsome celebrity and not only do they overcome their differences to work together, but they fall in love."

Hearing Didi describe it like that made my stomach clench. But maybe she was right - maybe the idea of Maya and I doing anything about our attraction was just as far-fetched as a fairy tale.

"They don't know that we have to put rules in place because it's just too messy otherwise. We've produced a lot of reality shows like this, and we've seen the damage that can be done when people who are forced together think they're acting rationally."

It took me a moment to process what Didi was even saying.

People who are forced together, thinking they're acting rationally when... they're not.

So maybe my feelings for Maya were just something that had come about from us working together. At least, that was the implication. It hadn't occurred to me to think of it like that. We had been doing so well together, too. Seeing Maya made my heart skip a beat and the way she smiled at me...

Could all of that be fake? Manufactured by the show?

"Alfie?" Didi said when I didn't reply.

"Sorry, sorry." I shook my head. "I hadn't thought about how the competition of it all might make things... seem more intense." Not *feel*. Definitely not feel. "Is that something that you see often then? I mean, Maya and I get on, obviously, and people love to make stuff up."

It felt like I was driving the point home almost a bit too much, so to lighten the mood, I added jokingly, "I'm sure that there's a slightly less popular #jaaron hashtag, too."

Didi laughed, but she nodded. "They don't even have to get on," she pointed out. "People can make a narrative out of almost anything." I could see her point. I was far from an expert in anything to do with couples, but even I could imagine that James and Aaron's arrogance would make them seem like an explosive relationship.

And maybe I was just making a narrative out of the time I'd spent with Maya. If the viewers could do it, then I probably could do it, too. Maya was the first woman I'd spent this much time with in ages. Or at least, the first woman who wasn't already dating someone else on the team.

"It happens," Didi continued. "Often we see these relationships flourish once the filming has stopped and then end just as abruptly. Either the press attention gets to them or else they realize that they never had that much in common to begin with."

"Right." I nodded like her words weren't cutting deep into my heart.

That perfectly described all of my worries and Didi didn't even know it. Getting to date Maya only for us to discover that we haven't got things in common and breaking up sounded... shit.

Considering that I'd never dated Maya before, the idea of losing her felt like a punch in the gut. Despite my internal turmoil, though, I couldn't let Didi know how much her words echoed with me.

"Eh, thanks. For talking with me. It's been... helpful."

It really hadn't at all been helpful, but I couldn't tell Didi that either.

Soon, the finale would start and somehow I now had more questions than I had started out with.

Chapter Sixteen

Maya

I had really never expected to make it to the final round of *Serves You Right*. Knowing I was one of the youngest, I'd assumed that the more experienced chefs would knock me out of the competition by the halfway point.

So when, weeks before filming even started, my boss had asked me to cater a motivational workshop the morning of filming, I'd agreed at once.

Now that the time had come, I was regretting all of my assumptions. The whole of my digestive system felt like one giant knot. I'd barely eaten and the scent of the fresh fruit I was cutting made me feel sick to my stomach.

"I'm sorry," I whined to Sophie, who was chopping bananas next to me and having to go twice as fast to make up for how slowly I was moving.

She'd already assured me that she understood. Anyone, she'd said, would be nervous about being in the finale.

Except that was the least of my anxieties! More than anything, I was worried about seeing Alfie again. I'd been so rude to him, telling him that we weren't even friends. And yet, it felt true to me. If we'd been anything more than mere acquaintances, Alfie would have told me about his girlfriend.

And he would have told me in a nicer way, to protect the feelings he must know I had! I'd said almost as much to him in my kitchen. There was no way he didn't know.

"Talk to me about something other than food," I begged. "I need a distraction."

The panicked look in Sophie's eyes made me laugh. As someone who worked in catering and was currently taking part in a cooking show, I could relate to not having a spread of topics to talk about. Still, Sophie grinned before shaking her head.

"Okay, okay. Not food," she repeated, like the words helped her unlock some secret space in her head where all the other topics of conversation were kept. "My sister told her boyfriend she wanted a pet for her birthday, thinking he'd get a dog or maybe a cat. I think she was even open to the idea of a bird." Sophie scrunched her nose up.

Sophie's weird dislike of birds was always amusing, especially when she had to cook them. "Anyway, he didn't get her any of those. Instead, he got her a pig. Like an actual pig. They live in an apartment."

That shook a laugh from me, freeing itself from the web of all my fears and sadness. "Oh, my God," I gasped. "Well at least she's not a chef, otherwise people would think she was just fattening it up to cook."

I could never have a food animal as a pet, it would be way too weird. "What is she going to do, don't pigs grow up to be pretty huge?" I'd read somewhere that even those 'miniature' pigs aren't really as small as people think they'll be.

It made me wonder about Alfie, whether he had ever wanted a pet. There'd certainly been no evidence of one when I'd visited his house. But I pushed that thought out of my head. The whole point of this conversation was not to keep thinking about Alfie.

"Well, I think she's looking at giving it away. Not that many in Salt Lake after a pig, who would have thought?" Sophie made a face, which just led me to laugh harder. "I think she might be also looking at getting rid of the boyfriend," she joked. "If you're looking for one, this one's fairly nice, comes with a pig."

My stomach twisted so hard that it hurt. I'd always been perfectly happy without a boyfriend, until now. But I didn't think that finding somebody else to date was going to make me miss Alfie any less.

Which just made me think about the fact that tonight, at the filming of the finale, might be the last time I'd get to see him. After all, I'd told him that we weren't friends. Why on earth would we hang out after filming had finished?

"No," I answered, shaking my head. "I think I'm going to stay single for a while. I need a break after spending so much energy on *Serves You Right*."

That seemed a pretty good answer but from the way Sophie frowned at me, I wasn't sure I'd completely masked my feelings. "It's really cool how you've done both," she informed me. "I kind of expected you to ask Ivan to swap you out of some of these shifts, but you've done both."

Sophie shook her head then, saying, "I couldn't have done that. It just seems to take so much energy! And I don't think I'd like being recognized either. Though, I don't imagine you do. Do people recognize you on the street now?"

It had happened a couple of times, but not often, so I shook my head. "I don't usually walk around with my hair down and in my chef's jacket," I pointed out. "I think when people see me with my hair in a bun and just wearing jeans and a t-shirt, they don't necessarily recognize me."

I looked quite different on the show, and that suited me fine. "I do have loads more Instagram followers now than I did before, though," I said. "That's been quite nice. I've even seen a few people try to replicate the dishes we've made on camera!"

"Oooh, that's cool," Sophie grinned. "You mostly just post pictures of food, don't you?" I nodded at that, because yeah, my Instagram was pretty exclusively pictures of different foods I'd cooked or liked.

"Do you get a lot of messages, though? I know that the #alfaya thing is pretty huge, do people send you weird stuff about that? Is there fanfiction? Oh, my God, imagine if there's fanfiction!"

I cringed inwardly. "I hope not," I muttered. It was bad enough that people thought Alfie and I were attracted to each other. Somehow, it felt ten times worse to imagine them writing out stories with perfect happy endings.

Happy endings that would never happen.

"Do you really think enough of our personality comes across on the show for people to write about us?" I asked. "I guess they can read interviews with Alfie to find out what he's like. But apart from knowing that I like food, I don't know what they'd say about me."

"I imagine they'd say you're very sweet, because you are," Sophie commented. "But also, the show has really pushed that. It makes you look... not that you're not nice, because you are, but they show a lot of the bits where you explain stuff to Alfie. I think it's cute, sure, but I also work with you, I know that's not what you're actually like."

That wasn't what I had expected; it made me frown a little.

"No, no, it's not bad," Sophie rushed to add. "I mean, it's better than them making you look like a villain, right? I think they've played up the cutesy thing between you and Alfie a lot and then the kind of competitive bit between James and Aaron. Your narrative is... sweeter."

I thought about that for a few minutes, trying to see it from Sophie's perspective. I did have to explain things to Alfie, because he knew a lot less about food than I did. But it was also true that Alfie let me explain. If I'd been paired with James, no matter how much more I knew than he did, I doubted I would've come across as sweet.

But that just threw me into confusion. Was our narrative sweet because Alfie and I were good together? Of course, even if it was, it didn't matter. Alfie was with somebody else. Despite how much it hurt, I was struggling to keep it in mind. It was like I wanted to forget, and so I did.

"Well, it's almost over," I said. "I'm sure people will slowly unfollow me on Instagram when they realize they're not getting exclusive pictures of Alfie Reeves." Hopefully, I would keep the few that were actually interested in cooking.

I forced a smile. "I'm looking forward to my life going back to normal," I lied.

"Are you, though?" Sophie asked, making me doubt my ability to lie very well. Yet, it didn't seem to be that she thought I was lying, and rather something else. "It's just that you've... I don't know. I'm not sure I'd say happier, but you've seemed kind of more content since you've been doing the competition?"

When I frowned, Sophie shrugged. "Yeah, stressed, too. But it suits you, the kind of pressure the show's been putting you under, I think. And what if you win? Even if you don't win, the publicity would help a lot to start your own business."

Sophie definitely had a point. If I didn't win, I would still want to do something to capitalize on the publicity. Maybe I should already be thinking about what it could be, but instead, all my thoughts had circled around Alfie and the heavy feeling in my heart.

"Yeah, you're right," I agreed, bumping Sophie gently with my shoulder. "Thanks. I think I needed that reminder." I wasn't going to let my emotions steal this opportunity from me. I still wanted to make the most of it, even if Alfie and I wouldn't stay friends after this was all over.

I was even feeling better enough that I could pick up the pace with our prep work. "Why don't you take a break?" I suggested. "I can finish the fruit and I'll call you when I need you for the next step."

Sophie did look at me a little skeptically, but she must have trusted me enough — or, at least, wanted a break enough — that she nodded. "Okay, yeah, but tell me if you do want more help," she told me, taking her apron off and setting it to one side.

After a moment's pause, Sophie surprised me by pulling me in a quick hug. "You're going to do awesomely today, I just know it," she informed me with a wide smile.

I squeezed back, my heart jumping up into my throat. It was the first time I'd thought of the finale with anything but dread. "Thanks, Sophie. And thanks for pushing me to enter in the first place. Without you, I never would've had the nerve."

We pulled apart, both grinning, and Sophie left me to get on with the rest of the fruit prep. While I chopped and sliced and seeded, I let my mind wander to what I might do with my publicity, whether I won or not.

It was enough to keep my thoughts off Alfie, at least most of the time. The nerves that still squirmed inside me would at least give me energy for the competition. Whether I could beat Aaron or not, I wanted to show off the best of my skills.

~*~

After the motivational breakfast was cleared away, I had too little time to really think about anything. My schedule had already been tight when my parents had called me to let me know they'd been invited to the finale, and did I want to grab a coffee before we were separated for filming?

Of course, I said 'yes'. Since work was always busy for me around the holiday season, I rarely had a good excuse to travel all the way home to see them. It had been over a year, and though we caught up over the telephone, it wasn't quite the same as seeing them both in person.

"Mom! Dad!" I greeted them at the airport with a hug each. I'd barely had the time to drive home and shower. No doubt my hair was even messier than usual from not having dried it properly. Luckily for me, the hair and make-up people on the show would fix it before it went out on national TV.

Mom definitely noticed, but she bit her lower lip not to say anything. "Let me take you to my favorite coffee place," I urged. "They do the most divine almond croissants."

"Sure," my dad said, nodding. As we drove, they caught me up on any immediate news that they might have shared if we'd phoned each other. It wasn't anything particularly thrilling but I still appreciated the way it included me into their lives.

Once there, my parents insisted that I let them pay before also buying us far too many almond croissants. "You said you liked them," Mom argued, making me shake my head. I did like them, but that hardly meant we had to get *all* of them.

But I understood, they were excited to see me. I was excited to see them, too.

"Obviously, we weren't going to say no, even if your mom's not too sure about being on the TV," Dad commented as we took seats by the window.

It startled me, because I hadn't given any thought to how this would be a decision for them. It had been presented by Didi as a done deal, of course, people's parents were going to come for the final.

That was when I realized that Alfie's parents wouldn't. He'd told me that he had no family left, which meant he'd be the only one of us who had to go through the ordeal alone.

It made my heart ache, and I wished that I could be there for him in some way. But I wasn't the right person. Maybe Didi would have invited Alfie's girlfriend, but he hadn't mentioned anything about that.

If they were still such a new couple, she might not want to appear on television.

"You'll be fine, Mom," I said, pushing my worries aside to concentrate on my parents. "What are you worried about?" Mom was a confident lady, it was hard for me to imagine what she might be scared of.

"It's just a bit intimidating," she shrugged. "I mean, watching you has been a delight, so that helps." The smile that my mom shot me made me instantly smile back. Reaching across the table, she gave my hand a squeeze. "We're very proud, honey. You have done so well."

Dad nodded, giving me an equally sweet smile. "And to think you've been paired with someone who doesn't eat vegetables. How is that boy surviving with no greens in his life?"

I laughed, affection for Alfie filling me to the brim before I could even think. It wasn't my place to be affectionate about Alfie's hatred of vegetables. It was his girlfriend's, whoever she was.

"Yeah," I agreed, "I don't know. But I haven't wanted to push him. He must get that all the time." I hoped his girlfriend was understanding, that she didn't mock Alfie for a preference he couldn't help.

But he wouldn't be with her if she did, right? Alfie struck me as far too confident to let anyone important belittle him like that.

"He's been great," I added, because it was true and because it would be weird for me not to even mention him. "I think him being so open about not being able to cook has helped me look good. People think I'm particularly nice for explaining things to him."

Mom gave a hum at that, like she was thinking of the perspective I had presented. "It's been enjoyable to watch," she decided. "I especially liked the challenge you two did about cooking easy things people could follow at home."

"Yes," my dad nodded. "Your mom even made those little pizza things for us," he informed me with a grin. "They were delicious. Yours might have looked a bit better, but only just."

The joke made Mom slap his arm lightly but she laughed, too. "I've never cooked something off the TV before," she admitted. "It was... kind of fun to have you be the one to teach me, even through the TV, so I imagine Alfie has enjoyed it, too."

My heart expanded in my chest, Mom's words rendering me almost speechless. After all the things I'd cooked off the TV, it was amazing to know that now I was the one teaching people at home how to follow along. Even my mom, who'd never really enjoyed cooking.

"Thanks, Mom," I managed to squeeze out. But then I thought about Alfie, about him standing all alone while the rest of us hugged and kissed our family members. If we won, I wanted there to be somebody to celebrate with Alfie. And if we lost, someone to thump his back and make him feel better.

Getting to my feet, I glanced towards the door. "Will you guys excuse me for a minute?" I asked. "There's something that I need to do."

Chapter Seventeen

Alfie

The days leading up to the finale somehow managed to feel like both forever and no time at all. Somehow, we were on Week Six of this show that I hadn't even wanted to be a part of. More importantly, somehow these six weeks had been some of the most exciting I'd had in years.

Hockey was always exciting, of course. I loved competition, loved playing, but this had been different. In some ways, at least. It was still a competition. That bit I knew how to deal with. The level of competitiveness that I felt was probably a bit too much, especially with having wanted to prepare beforehand.

I'd even gone so far as to read some cooking blogs and watch the Food Network. Something I instantly thought that Maya would enjoy knowing. But then it struck me that maybe she wouldn't.

We weren't even friends, right?

Hell, if I believed what Didi said, everything I felt for Maya might just be a result of being on the show. Feelings ran high, I got that. It felt real to me, though. Then again, there was no knowing for certain.

That played on my mind a lot as I drove to the studio.

There was no time to chat with Maya that day, not that I would have known what to say anyway. Thankfully, everyone was rushed off to hair and makeup, getting ready for the finale.

It felt like a different sort of buzz than the normal competition days. The closest I could liken it to was playing in the playoffs, nearing the Stanley Cup, practically being able to see it. I was hopeful that this would be a bit more successful than the Pumas' chances for the Cup had been lately.

"For today's challenge," Alix announced as we finally started filming. "We've got some special guests. You will be cooking for the people who matter the most in your lives - your families."

Oh.

Well, this would be awkward.

I glanced at Maya next to me, watching her chew her lower lip. Even without having spoken to her, I felt like I could practically hear her worry. "It's alright," I promised quietly. "I'll just borrow yours," I teased, hoping it'd break the ice between us.

She shot me a small smile, one that made my heart turn over in my chest. I tried to push the feeling aside, telling myself that it was only the excitement of the competition that was making me react that way.

"I picked my parents up from the airport this afternoon," she said, "they're excited to meet you." Older couples filed into the room, one pair going over to James, kissing him on both cheeks before shaking hands with Aaron.

I watched, feeling my stomach churn. Shit, this was going to be so awkward when nobody came over to greet me like that. Not for the first time, I wished my Nana could've been here to see this. She would've loved Maya, I had no doubt.

Mostly, though, I knew that Maya would feel bad. While losing my Nana had been hard, it was something I'd slowly accepted. Not having any family sucked, sure, but I was kind of used to it.

What I knew of Maya - and whether we were or weren't friends, I did now feel like I knew her quite well - was enough to know she would feel sad that I had no one coming to the finale. Maya feeling sad bothered me a lot more than not having anyone there.

"Alfie," Alix smiled at me and I was readying myself for the apology I'd inevitably get about there being no one here for me. But that wasn't what happened. "We know that you don't have any immediate family that we could invite, but Maya," and there she glanced at Maya and so did I, surprise on my face.

"Maya suggested we invite the family you do have." And with that, the door opened and in came Luke, Will, Levi, Chuck, and Olle. "We had to limit it to only five," Alix explained.

"So they picked the best ones," Levi grinned at me as the guys all came over to pat me on the back.

It was hard to believe that for a second time in as many weeks they had managed to keep a secret. But more than that, my heart swelled with affection at knowing that Maya had organized this, that she'd made sure I had someone here even when I didn't even know I'd want that.

Turning to Maya as the guys were seated, I gave her a soft smile. "Thank you," I said just as Alix announced a commercial break.

Maya's answering grin was bright and happy. It made me forget for a moment that she'd said we weren't friends. After all, would she have bothered to do this for me if I was just an acquaintance? It didn't seem likely.

"I didn't want you to feel sad," she explained, mimicking my own thoughts so exactly that, for a moment, all I could do was blink at her. "And you said the guys were basically your brothers, right?" I nodded. "So, I got Nadine to give me Chuck's number and I called Didi to ask if we had to invite just two people, or if it could be more..."

She trailed off, shrugging like it was no big deal. But it was. Knowing that she'd gone to all that effort made something fizz inside me.

"We're coming back from the commercial in three, two, one," one of the producers called, reminding me that we were filming live. Playing hockey live felt very different from this, but I tried to focus on the competition, all we had to do was win.

Yet, the way my heart twisted at Maya's words, it was practically impossible to remind myself that everyone's eyes were on us. "You did... all of this for me?" I asked. It felt almost unreal. No one had ever gone through so much effort just for me. Not when they didn't have to. Hell, even when they did have to.

Maya was the loveliest person I had ever met.

And all I wanted to do was kiss her.

Maya frowned, looking up at me with confusion in her eyes. "Well, yeah," she said. "Who else would I be doing it for? I mean, I'm sure Didi would say it's better for the show to have somebody here for you than have to explain why no one is. But I didn't do it because I thought the show would be better."

Glancing back at the camera, Maya shifted slightly, coming closer. "I know I said we weren't friends," she said, voice suddenly low and sincere, "but I didn't really mean it. I was just - startled, that you had a girlfriend and you hadn't mentioned it. But no hard feelings, Alfie, really."

No hard feelings.

Except all of my feelings were hard.

Oh. That sounded kind of wrong. But also probably not untrue. But it wasn't just hard feelings. It was easy feelings, too. In fact, I would go as far as to say it was *all* of my feelings.

"Maya," I drew out slowly. It was like no one else was there at all, like nothing mattered but her. "I don't." I should have told her the truth, I shouldn't have pretended. It clearly had hurt her and that was so far from what I wanted to do. "I don't have a girlfriend."

And then, before I could even think of how stupid a thing to do this was, my lips were on Maya's.

When she gasped against me, I didn't know if it was from what I'd said or from the kiss. But she didn't pull away.

Instead, I felt her head tilt, her lips fitting even more perfectly against mine.

That was all I had time to notice before a loud cheer went up from somewhere on my left. Fuck. I recognized those voices, and it was impossible not to slam back into reality.

I pulled away, my gaze snapping to Maya's wide eyes. "Oh no! Alfie, what do we do?"

And wasn't that the question?

Guilt pounded through me. There were so many reasons why I shouldn't have kissed Maya, but that list increased exponentially when considering where we were. Live on air. Watched by God only knew how many people. Not to mention that we'd signed contracts that specifically banned us from intimacy.

We were going to get disqualified. And it was all my fault.

Yet, none of that stopped me from wanting to kiss Maya again. At least I managed to resist it this time. I might have already cost us the competition.

Alix spoke then, breaking the startled silence the rest of the crew seemed to have fallen into. "We still have a challenge for you," the hostess reminded us. "So today we…"

It was so hard to focus on Alix as she explained the different types of foods we'd be cooking today. All I could think about was how good Maya had felt against me, how soft her lips had been, how much I wanted to see what other sounds I could make her give.

If she'd even want that.

Kissing Maya in front of everyone like this... it was a mistake. I was stupid and we very well might be cooking for nothing. From the smug look on James' face, he seemed to already believe that he and Aaron had won. And I couldn't even convince myself he was wrong.

Maya deserved so much better than this.

So much better than *me*.

I risked a glance toward Maya, who looked almost as stunned as I felt. Her cheeks had flushed pink, her lips definitely looking redder than they had before I'd kissed her.

But she didn't look angry. At least, I didn't think so. I'd never seen Maya get angry at anything, and I didn't want to start now.

The camera people moved around us, the motion catching Maya's attention, making her turn her head to follow them.

"I... guess we cook?" Maya asked, sounding uncertain. "I know my parents have watched the show, and you said you were watching it with the team, right? So maybe we could make something with elements we've used before, but put them in a new context?"

The whole thing felt surreal.

Focusing on what Maya was saying and not on the curve of her lower lip was a genuine challenge. But no one had told us we were disqualified yet. Not that they could, right? They couldn't disqualify us before the end of the show, what would they even air if they did?

So we should cook. "Yeah." I nodded dumbly, before actually thinking about what Maya had said. I might have already ruined our chances at winning, yes, but what if I hadn't? Then we still needed to beat James and Aaron. We could do this, if we just worked as a team.

I tried to not think that, not only might I have gotten us disqualified, but also that I'd kissed Maya in front of her parents. And my team. And literally everyone watching the show right now.

The show, as they said, needed to go on.

"Okay, well, we started with deep-fried ball things. Can we ball and deep fry something else as our... ah-tree?" That wasn't it.

I watched Maya try to restrain a giggle. She pressed her lips together, her shoulders shaking for a moment before she recovered enough to answer my question. "Entrée. Yeah, there are loads of things we can deep fry. Maybe arancini? It's like deep-fried risotto."

That sounded pretty good, actually, so I nodded.

"Then we could do a crab pasta dish? You liked the crab when I made it before, and we can make a nice sauce for it." They'd given us longer to complete this challenge than they ever had before, and I could practically see Maya stretching her ambitions to fit the amount of time we had available.

There were a lot of things I would be taking away from this competition. Mostly, feelings towards Maya. But also, apparently, the fact that crab was now something I was willing to eat. How much of that was because Maya cooked it, though, I wasn't sure.

"Can we make some kind of mustard sauce for it? And then for the dessert that leaves us with blueberries and... birthday cake?" Of all the things we had cooked, there weren't a lot that would work in the desert. At least I didn't think so anyway. "There's sweet pizzas, aren't there? Blueberry birthday cake pizza?"

Maybe that was just a string of words, actually.

"I don't know about specifically *birthday cake* pizza," Maya admitted. "But blueberry pizza is definitely something we can do. White chocolate ganache to represent the cheese, watermelon puree for the tomato sauce, and blueberries on top!"

Maya sounded so excited about it. I couldn't help but feel a little sad to think this might be the last time we cooked together.

Or maybe it wouldn't. Not knowing was keeping me on edge, my anxiety far worse than it had been before any hockey match.

"That's quite a lot, but I think they gave us enough time," Maya observed. "And I think your friends and my parents will appreciate it. That's the important thing now."

It made my chest ache. I didn't want Maya to only be cooking for our friends and family. I wanted her to believe we could win this competition! But how could she, when we didn't even know if we'd be allowed to compete?

I wanted to promise her that whatever the money for winning the competition was, I'd just give it to her. But that was stupid. For one, I was very sure that Maya would refuse it.

Still, my stomach twisted at the idea that my stupid actions, my inability to stop my impulses, might have cost Maya her dream of owning her own business. Yet under all of that, there was still such a draw within me. A draw towards her. I had to push my hands in my pockets briefly just not to reach out and touch her.

"Well," I cleared my throat. "I am pretty good at chopping now," I told Maya, giving her a soft grin.

She nodded. "And you're an expert cornflake-crusher," she added, making me laugh. My emotions warred inside me, from pleasure that we could still share laughter and good memories to guilt that I might have ruined all those weeks of hard work.

But Maya had set us a goal, and we were both determined that, whatever kept us from winning, it wasn't going to be a lack of effort.

So we started work, Maya instructing me in the easier tasks while she took anything that involved complicated cooking. We fell into sync so easily that I practically forgot James and Aaron and the cameras were even in the room.

As we went about cooking, I kept stealing glances at Maya.

She looked so good, a strand of hair falling over her face, making me want to reach out and brush it away.

Whatever happened next, whether we lost, got disqualified or anything else, I knew I would miss doing this with Maya.

This competition had involved so many weird ups and downs. When the guys had signed me up to it, I couldn't possibly have imagined being in the finale (that I may have ruined), cooking alongside Maya and feeling almost like I knew what I was doing.

Working with Maya, being a team with Maya, it was the best thing that had come out of this competition for me.

And I'd tell her as much the moment we weren't on camera.

If she even wanted to talk to me.

Shit.

There was a chance that I had ruined Maya's dream. Because of one stupid kiss. Because of not being able to control myself.

Watching her cook, it was like watching the best players slide across the ice. She was so effortless, so full of passion. All I could do was hope that I could assist, despite having already ruined our chances by committing a foul.

I just hoped that she could forgive me.

Chapter Eighteen

Maya

I couldn't think about the fact Alfie had kissed me. I couldn't think about what it might mean - either for us or for our position in the competition. If I stopped to process any of it, the uncertainty was going to eat me alive.

So I did what I do best. I cooked. Pulling together elements from the dishes we'd made together felt like a fitting tribute. And the three-course meal I'd planned was complicated enough that it barely gave me time to breathe.

Alfie worked with me brilliantly, handing me things almost before I'd asked for them, and chopping anything I pushed in his direction.

By the time we'd pulled everything together, I felt certain that we couldn't have done any more. We'd watched, my heart in my throat, as the judges tried first our dishes and then the plates presented by James and Aaron.

They didn't say much. Alix explained that they were going to deliberate privately in front of the cameras before coming to a conclusion and announcing the winner of *Serves You* *Right*.

In the meantime, Didi was filming a segment for the audience and so we were allowed to take a little break.

Alfie shepherded me out of the building, neither of us exchanging a word until we were certain there were no more cameras.

I didn't know what to say. Part of me wanted to throw my arms around his neck and kiss him properly, the way I hadn't been able to when the Pumas started cheering for us earlier.

But I didn't know whether that was what Alfie wanted. Sure, he'd kissed me, and told me that he didn't have a girlfriend, but did that mean I could count on him wanting something long-term?

"Why did you make up a girlfriend?" I asked, genuinely unsure. "Was it - Were you afraid I was getting too close?"

He bit his lower lip, looking down at our feet. "Kind of," Alfie admitted, making my insides twist unpleasantly. Before I could self-indulge in what that might mean, though, Alfie was speaking again. This time, though he did look up at me, I could tell that he struggled to meet my eyes.

"I was afraid that I'd get us disqualified," he told me before shaking his head. "Fuck, Maya, I'm so stupid. What if I *have* gotten us disqualified? I shouldn't have kissed you, I know. I'm so sorry. I just... it was dumb. This competition, it's so important to you and here I am, just messing it up."

It was no use pretending that I wasn't worried about that. But still, I objected to Alfie's interpretation of it. "You're not stupid," I insisted. "Of course you're not. I've wanted to kiss you, too, so many times."

Admitting it made my heart drum louder in my chest. But Alfie had kissed me. If there was ever a time to recklessly declare my feelings, it was now.

"Alfie, you're amazing. You're so sweet and so supportive. Obviously, I don't *want* to be disqualified, but if we are, it'll be worth it if -"

Here was the big point. It would be worth it if Alfie wanted more than just one kiss. And I still wasn't completely sure if that was true.

Shaking my head, I carried on. "If we're disqualified, I won't blame you for kissing me."

"But you should.," Alfie frowned. "It's my fault. I... shouldn't have." That made my stomach turn again, did he mean he shouldn't have kissed me? Whatever emotions flashed across my face made Alfie rush in with more words.

"Not because I didn't want to! I... fuck, Maya, I really did want to. I still want to." And then, Alfie was there, so close to me that his body pressed against mine. Without any hesitation, my arms came up, wrapping around him as I tiptoed to help our lips meet.

This was different from the kiss we'd shared earlier. It was harder, more passionate. No one was watching now so Alfie could lick his way into my mouth, teeth lightly grazing over my bottom lip.

I gasped again, feeling Alfie's breath mingle with mine. He tasted sweet, like the blueberries I knew he'd grabbed while we were decorating our dessert pizza, but there was a spiciness under it that was entirely his own.

We kissed for ages, until my lungs burned from the lack of oxygen and I had to reluctantly pull back. "I wanted you to," I whispered. "Maybe not right then, but I've wanted you to for ages."

Now that Alfie had kissed me breathless, I felt light-headed. It was hard to remember that there was any potential downside. "It was worth it," I said. "Even if we get disqualified, even if this is the only time it can happen, it will still be worth it."

Then I giggled. "But I hope it isn't the only time." I wanted it to happen again, not just right now but for days and weeks in the future.

Alfie gave me a look that seemed so full of concern that all I could do was bring my hand up to his cheek, to stroke my hand over it, like I could pet it away. The way he leaned into my touch made my heart race.

"I'd definitely like to kiss you some more," Alfie promised. "It's just... this means so much to you, Maya. And we've done so great! It's stupid of me to have risked it all." Alfie paused, chewing on his lower lip briefly. "Well, maybe not stupid. I don't regret kissing you. Maybe I should, but I don't."

My heart lifted at those words. "I'm glad. I wouldn't want you to regret it." I tiptoed up, pressing my lips to Alfie's once more in a soft, chaste kiss. Even that was enough to make me stop breathing for a moment.

"I don't know what this is going to be, between us," I said, the fear I had once felt about admitting my feelings vanished in the intensity of the moment. "But whatever it will be, I want to find out. I want that more than I want the money to start my own business."

It was true. If I had to pick, I would pick Alfie. After all, there were other ways I could save up enough money. There weren't any other Alfies out there in the world.

"About that," Alfie said with a small frown. "I know that your first reaction is going to be to say no, but think about it, okay? If we do get disqualified, I'd like to help you with setting up your own business. I have the money." My eyes widened; Alfie couldn't be serious.

He didn't let me say as much. Not straight away. His hand came up to brush over my cheek, just the way I had done to him. "It can be a loan, it can be anything, I just... I want you to have your dreams, Maya."

My stomach swirled with such intense emotions. This wasn't just a casual thing that Alfie was talking about. If he was willing to loan me money, he must be looking for something long-term.

But I knew that I couldn't let him do it. It would be bad enough to accept a loan from a friend. I wasn't going to complicate a brand new relationship, if that was even what we were.

"It's so generous of you, Alfie," I said. He looked at me with such pleading eyes that I couldn't dismiss his offer out of hand.

"I'll think about it, if we get disqualified. But only then. If we lose because James and Aaron were better -" The thought made me feel almost sick.

The way Alfie scrunched his nose up, I knew he wasn't very pleased with that idea either. "I think that's worse than being disqualified," he informed me and the intensity of that statement made me laugh. God, I hoped we didn't get disqualified but I also didn't want to lose.

Somehow, the competitiveness that Alfie felt was rubbing off on me. "It's true, you can catch it through kissing," Alfie agreed when I said as much. "But I have the one known cure."

When I raised my eyebrow at that, Alfie grinned. "It's more kissing."

I laughed, the sound so light and joyful that it made me realize just how differently I felt about things now than I had as little as a week ago. I'd tried so hard to keep my feelings about Alfie to myself, it was a relief to know that I didn't have to anymore.

"We can definitely do more kissing," I agreed. But just as Alfie swept closer, I held up a hand to hold him back. "I think, right now, we should get back inside. Otherwise, we might get carried away."

It was bad enough that Alfie had kissed me on camera. We could, honestly, say that it was the first time and that we hadn't been lying about it all these weeks. Maybe that would help our case with the producers.

But if they caught us doing more than kissing, I felt we'd definitely be disqualified. We had to show our faces.

"Maybe..." I hesitated, suddenly shy. "Maybe you could say hi to my parents?"

"Oh.." Alfie frowned and for a moment I almost rushed in to say that, of course, he didn't have to. A few kisses hardly meant he needed to meet my parents. It was probably too early, right? All the thoughts that rushed through my head were about how I was asking for too much, how Alfie would say he wasn't ready.

But then a brilliant smile blossomed across his face.

"Yeah, I'd very much like that," he nodded. "I'd introduce you to the guys, but you've already met them. And also they're dicks." He grinned. Then, Alfie reached out to take my hand, giving it a squeeze.

Butterflies fluttered inside me, filling me up with energy that practically tingled in my fingers. I had no idea what my parents were going to think about Alfie kissing me on TV, but at least they'd been watching him on the show for six weeks. He wasn't a stranger.

Still, anxiety curdled through me as we made our way back into the studio. At any moment, I expected someone to come over and tell us that we weren't welcome. What if they'd disqualified us in our absence?

But nobody approached us. And once we reached the room we were filming in, Alix gave us a nod and flashed ten fingers at us, letting us know how long we had before they were ready to start up again.

Ten minutes might be more time than Alfie really wanted to spend getting introduced to my family. But he'd agreed now, so I led the way over to where my mom and dad were sitting.

"Mom, Dad, I thought you should actually meet Alfie. Alfie, these are my parents, Shawn and Dana."

"Ma'am, sir." Alfie nodded at them both individually, making my stomach twist with butterflies. He sounded so polite, it instantly occurred to me just how well his nana must have raised him.

My parents seemed to appreciate it, too. Dad took a step forward holding his hand out to Alfie. "It's a pleasure to meet you, Alfie," he said and my mom gave a noise of agreement. "The food you and Maya prepared was absolutely delicious, I don't know how the judges will make their choice."

"It really was," Mom told me, reaching out to give my arm a squeeze. "It's much more tense being here than watching it on the TV," she informed us all, making my dad chuckle.

"She's not wrong, but I guess you must be quite used to pressure, Alfie? Your work's all about competition."

"It is, kind of," Alfie nodded. "This, truthfully, feels more scary."

I shook my head, still unable to understand how a kitchen could possibly be a scarier place than an ice rink filled with hockey players. "Maybe that's why we work so well together, we're both scared of what the other person can do," I teased.

My parents knew I wasn't interested in hockey, so they both laughed, while Alfie just gave me a smile that seemed to reflect my own feelings. It was weird to think that he might consider me just as brave as I thought him.

"It's a shame it's over," I admitted. "I've enjoyed the challenge of cooking to actually impress people."

"Well, maybe you can keep impressing me with it," Alfie joked. "I'm very easy to be impressed with cooking," he added for my parents' sake, though from the way Dad chuckled, I was pretty sure they didn't need to be told.

"We do watch the show," Dad pointed out and I could swear Alfie's cheeks turned slightly pink at that.

Mom, thankfully, stepped in then. Or well, I thought it'd be helpful until I heard what she said. "You do know that kissing Maya like that, live on air, it's going to make people talk." But as she said it, my mom's eyes fell down to our hands, Alfie's still holding mine.

"I know," Alfie said, shaking his head. "It was... stupid. I've already apologized to Maya. I shouldn't have done that. Your daughter means a lot to me, ma'am, I can promise you that."

I could have swooned right there on the spot. It was the sweetest thing anybody had ever said to me. Mom melted almost as obviously as I did, her gaze darting between Alfie and my Dad.

Surely, it was way too soon to be thinking we might have a relationship that lasted as long as my parents' had? But nonetheless, a little vista of what the future might be like if we did, played in my mind's eye.

"That was honestly the first time anything like that has happened," I said. "I hope they'll take that into account. But if not, well, it's been a great experience and it's got my name out there. That'll have to be enough."

And yet, it was more than I'd thought possible when Sophie made me send in my audition tape.

"You must be looking forward to not having to film anymore, though?" I suggested to Alfie. "You can get back to all hockey all the time."

He gave a small hum, like it was a question he had to consider. Then, almost sheepishly, Alfie gave a shrug. "Yeah, I'm not going to lie, I don't think I'll miss cooking on the TV. It's been nice, but it's only the fact that I got paired with you that's made it nice."

That, too, made me smile.

"Maya's proved herself to be a good teacher," Dad commented, his tone full with pride that made my affection swell.

"She really has been," Alfie agreed with a nod. "As you know, I'm very far from a foodie, but Maya's passion for food is hard not to admire. She's even gotten me to try stuff I'd never heard of."

I beamed. A familiar longing tugged at my heart. I wanted to be able to introduce Alfie to more foods. And not just that, I wanted to learn to cook them in ways that he would genuinely enjoy.

For the first time, there was nothing painful in the thought. Alfie and I would keep seeing each other, even after we stopped filming. We would have days together without any cameras. I'd be able to learn more about his past, and show him more of my cooking.

That thought was so sweet that I genuinely didn't mind if we were disqualified from *Serves You Right*. The fact that I'd met Alfie at all was prize enough for me.

Chapter Nineteen

Alfie

Meeting Maya's parents was surprisingly nice. It almost eased my nerves about the competition. It didn't completely ease the guilt I felt about potentially having ruined the competition. But every time it twisted inside me, I turned to look at Maya.

She looked stunning, cheeks flushed just a little. Knowing that after this, no matter how things went, I could kiss Maya again made me feel better. Sure, I still wanted us to win, but first, we'd have to find out if we were going to get disqualified.

Just before going back live on air, Didi called us over.

"So, I've had a conversation with the execs," she told us, my hand gripping Maya's a little tighter. "We've decided not to disqualify you two."

It felt like I suddenly remembered how to breathe.

"You're not?" I heard myself ask.

"We're not," Didi confirmed. "The rule is in place to make sure no unfair practices go on and the execs did not feel that two of the contestants being involved is worth disqualification. Truthfully, maybe it'd be different if this wasn't the finale but..."

The way Didi paused, I was sure there was something else, but then she just grinned at the two of us. "We've all been team #alfaya since like episode one anyway."

I heard Maya gasp from beside me. Turning my head, I could see even more color rise into her cheeks. Maybe I would have blushed, too, but I was just so happy that Maya still had a chance to win.

"Oh, I'm so glad," Maya said quickly. "Thank you, Didi. And, I guess, thank the executive producers for me, if that seems appropriate?"

Frankly, I wasn't sure they needed to be *thanked* for not disqualifying us, but I was hardly going to argue.

"We'll be ready in a few minutes," Didi informed us, giving Maya a quick glance. "You might want to get make-up to reapply your lipstick before we start filming."

She left us with that, Maya flushing scarlet and lifting a hand to her lips as if she would be able to feel whatever damage our kissing had done.

"So now we find out whether we did enough to win," she said, squeezing my hand that was still wrapped around hers.

It was hard to feel too worried about the result when minutes ago we hadn't even known if we'd be allowed to be considered. Still, losing to James would suck. I hoped that we'd done enough to get this victory. Maya deserved to win, I believed that with all my heart.

The make-up people were quick. Before too long, we were lining up to start filming again. Maya and I had finally stopped holding hands, but I stood close enough to her that I could let my pinky finger brush against her hand every so often.

"Welcome back!" Alix exclaimed into the camera. "After a dramatic day, we are ready to announce the pair to win *Serves You Right*."

She went on to talk about how the season had been, about the different challenges. It was almost impossible to focus on any of it, my heart pounding loud enough that I was surprised the microphone wasn't picking it up.

Beside me, Maya was actually trembling. It brought home to me how much more this mattered to her than it did to me. Even though I obviously wanted us to win, it wouldn't change my life.

But if Maya won the money, she'd actually be able to fulfill a dream of hers. It reminded me of when I'd been waiting for the draft announcement at 17, to find out whether I'd made it onto a team or not.

Winning this money was like Maya's NHL.

But Alix still drew the process out, asking Aaron what he'd do with the money if he won. I didn't even listen. He was already a head chef, and I didn't care whether he wanted to open his own restaurant or bring out a cookbook or whatever else.

I expected the question to then be thrown to Maya, so when Alix addressed me, it took me a moment to realize. "Alfie?" she repeated and I blinked.

"Sorry?"

"I asked what it would mean to you to win," Alix said, her tone patient like she didn't mind that I hadn't been listening, even though we were live on air.

Thankfully, even if I hadn't been prepared for the question, I did know the answer. Spending the last however long thinking that we would be disqualified had certainly given me some perspective on it.

"Um, well, it's a bit of a mix, I guess. I want us to win because I think Maya deserves us to," I answered honestly. "She's worked really hard and truthfully, I know I was a bit of a blow as the celebrity to be paired up with. I can't cook, I don't even know half of the ingredients that Maya names." There was a general chuckle from the people in the audience at that.

"But apart from that, I do want to win for me, too. I've got to the finale! Me! The guy who doesn't even eat vegetables. And it'd really show my team what as--eh, what..." My brain drew a blank on any fitting descriptor that wasn't a swear word. "Anyway, it would be pretty awesome for me. But mostly, I want us to win because Maya's so great."

Glancing at Maya beside me, I caught her looking at me with such gratitude and admiration in her eyes that it took my breath away. And yet, everything I had said was simply true. More than anything, we deserved to win because Maya was exceptionally passionate. She'd even got me interested in food!

"And you, Maya? Do you want to win for Alfie?" Alix asked, her tone lightly teasing.

Maya's gaze darted to me, then back to Alix. "Well, not really," she admitted. "I know Alfie would be delighted if we won. It would mean the world to him to get to donate his winnings to a charity that supports children who don't have enough access to food."

I'd never even said that out loud, but Maya was right, I would love it. "But if James and Aaron win, that money will still go to a good cause," Maya pointed out. "And I've gotten to know Alfie well enough to know he'd still be glad, even if it was James' winnings and not his."

She licked her lips, shrugging one shoulder. "I want to win for me. Because I've loved being on *Serves You Right* so much. Challenging myself to come up with new dishes every week has been so exciting.

"If I win, I'll be able to open my own catering firm, and I'll get to design my own menus all the time. I want that, more than anything."

Alix seemed very pleased with our answers and, from behind the cameras, so did Didi. James was the last person who was asked what it would mean for him to win. Mostly he just talked about how much he wanted to 'give back', whatever that meant. Either way, Maya was right, I didn't really care which of us donated money to charity.

But I still wanted to beat James.

Finally, we were ready to hear who'd actually won. If I'd thought my heart had been beating hard before, it felt like it might try to jump out of my chest now. My hand reached for Maya's, not even in a romantic way, but just because I felt a bit like I needed her hand in mine.

Alix was talking again about how everyone had done so amazingly, how the judges had loved the food but there was almost a buzzing in my ears. And then, through it, I heard.

"And the winners of *Serves You Right* are... Maya and Alfie!"

For a second, everything froze, my heart skipping a beat and the world going white around me. And then Luke cheered, the rest of the Pumas quickly joining in. I grabbed Maya to me, wrapping my arms around her waist and lifting her up and up.

She threw her head back, looking so beautiful and so *thrilled*. Just knowing that I had been a part of that would have been enough of a reward for me.

The guys crowded around us, Maya's parents hanging back from the fray but clapping so hard it must have hurt.

I brought Maya carefully back down to earth, only for the Pumas to hoist her up between them. My chest felt so full of emotion that I could hardly untangle one feeling from another.

Watching the guys who were my brothers celebrating with Maya was the best feeling in the world.

Everything after that was a bit of a swirl of activity. More interviews about how we felt, some more comments from the judges and then the final credits rolled. It wasn't until Didi announced that it was a wrap that things really sank in.

I let Maya celebrate with her parents, smiling at her across the room.

After talking to Didi a bit and having both James and Aaron congratulate me, I finally found my way to Maya. Her parents shot me a smile, before nudging Maya's shoulder so she'd turn to see that I was behind her.

"Congratulations," I grinned when her parents walked off to give us some privacy.

"Oh, Alfie, I can hardly believe it," she gushed. Her face was lit up with the biggest smile I'd ever seen as she reached out, twining her fingers through mine and pulling me close enough that I could smell the sweet scent of her perfume.

She looked up at me, her eyes clear and sparkling. "I couldn't have done it without you, you know. Nobody else would have supported me as brilliantly as you have."

I wasn't sure whether that was really true. "We worked so well together," she continued. "You always got what I wanted to do and helped me make it better."

That was probably true. Maya and I had worked together exceptionally well and somehow in that, I was pretty sure I'd fallen in love with her. This wasn't the right time to tell her as much, but I did wonder if perhaps she already knew.

"I think I know what you want now, too," I informed her, my grin widening. One of my hands snuck around, pulling Maya in closer against me. "Can I kiss you, Maya? Now that we know for sure no one's going to disqualify us."

Maya beamed, her body settling against mine. She tiptoed up, claiming my mouth with a soft kiss that entirely answered the question I had asked. The Pumas still cheered, but this time, we were able to ignore them.

I only pulled back because getting any more passionate in front of Maya's parents felt a little weird. But I hoped that, soon, we'd be able to find a time and place that was only for the two of us.

"We should go out for a meal, to celebrate," Maya said. "But... maybe tonight we could do something just for the two of us? I'd be happy to cook you something."

"I would offer to cook, but.." We both laughed before I shook my head. "But maybe you should let me order some food. You've done so much cooking. You've cooked us to victory!"

And that was going to take a while to sink in. I had won a cooking competition.

"Oh!" My eyes widened. "I won the bet!" I exclaimed. At Maya's confused frown, my smile widened even more. "The team bet I would go out at different weeks and I was the only one who bet on me to win! We're going to have the best takeaway this city has to offer."

Maya's delighted laugh and shining eyes more than made up for all the chirping I'd endured about my lack of cooking talent.

"You're going to regret that offer, Alfie Reeves," she warned me. "I'm going to order so many things that you've never heard of."

She tiptoed once again, pressing her lips to mine. "But I promise, if you don't like them, you don't have to eat more than one bite."

There was so much affection in me that I felt almost overwhelmed with it. I wanted Maya to order all the food in the city if that was what she desired. More than that, hearing her promise to only have me try the food and knowing that she meant it too, it just made my affection grow.

During all of this process, Maya had never tried to force me to eat something, she'd never pushed it. Yet, I'd tried more foods with her than I ever had with anyone else. Not all of it I liked, but there was more than I'd expected to like.

Maya had managed to do something no one ever had - make me want to try different foods.

"For you? I'll take a bite of everything," I promised.

Maya squeezed my hand, the happiness on her face almost more intense than in that moment that we'd won. Almost, but not quite. That was fair enough: winning was a big deal!

"I want to learn to make the things you love, too," she said. "I mean, I can already make pizza pretty well, but there must be other things? Or just things that you want to try."

All my fears about Maya and I being too different too incompatible, dissolved in an instant. I should have known that Maya loved cooking so much that she'd find a way to enjoy cooking for me, even if my list of preferred ingredients was shorter than most people would like.

"You're too good for me," I informed her seriously. In many ways, I really thought she was. No one had cared about me the way Maya did. Ever, possibly. My nana had been a wonderful person and she had loved me, but I knew that she hadn't chosen to raise her daughter's kid. She'd been fantastic at it, but it hadn't been her choice.

Maya, though? She had chosen me.

Leaning in, I pressed a soft kiss against Maya's lips. "I'm going to try very hard to earn you being so good to me," I promised.

She looked as if she wanted to argue, so I kissed her again, loving the way her warm cheek brushed my nose as I leaned in.

It was Maya who pulled back this time, the words spilling from her almost before she'd completely finished kissing me. "I'm not too good, Alfie. We're both so great together! I'm a much better chef with you than I am without you."

And I was much better at trying new foods, so maybe that was why we worked out so well.

"You don't need to earn me. You've already got me."

That sounded lovely, that I might already have Maya. It didn't, however, mean that I shouldn't still do everything in my power to earn her. I was going to treat Maya so well that she'd want to let me keep her.

"Come on," I said with a grin. "Let's go celebrate with everyone and then go back to my place. We can even watch *Serves You Right*," I joked. Or well, perhaps it'd be a little interesting. I didn't think I'd mind seeing our first kiss on camera, especially now that we knew we weren't going to get disqualified over it.

Whatever happened from now on, Maya and I would be in charge of it.

Chapter Twenty

Maya

It was as if all my dreams had come true at once. Not only had Alfie and I won *Serves You Right*, but we'd also made such promises to each other that I could hardly doubt we would be happy for a long time to come.

We spent as much time as we could together, mostly at Alfie's house, but sometimes in my apartment with Nadine. We exchanged favorite restaurants and took turns picking what film to watch or what music to listen to.

The fact that we had very different taste in both didn't matter at all. If I knew Alfie liked something, I was happy to watch it just so that I would know more about him. And he said the same for me.

Naturally, the fuss about #alfaya only got more intense once our fans had watched the final episode. When we went out, people would stop us in the street to congratulate us, and to ask whether we'd been in a secret relationship all along.

Even though we told them no, I'm not sure anyone actually believed us.

A week later, the day we would have been filming, I arrived at Alfie's with a grocery bag full of ingredients.

"Right, Alfie Reeves," I announced, after kissing him hello, "our challenge today is to brainstorm a vegetable dish that you might actually like. I've brought lots of things you like, plus a vegetarian cookbook we can go through for inspiration."

Seeing that Alfie looked worried, I rested my hand on his arm. "I'm not going to force you to eat it all if you hate it," I promised. "But I really think that there must be a way of cooking at least one vegetable that you'll actually enjoy."

"Okay," Alfie drew out slowly. "But I will only commit to one," he informed me. It was, I thought, most likely a joke. Still, I wouldn't force Alfie to eat anything he didn't want to and I knew he knew that, too.

Once we were in the kitchen, Alfie let me go about getting things we would need. It pleased me that he just let me take over his kitchen. We'd talked about it before, about how Alfie just didn't really know how to utilize the space best. And, well, I loved a kitchen, especially one as big as Alfie's.

"Am I going to be on chopping duties?" Alfie asked, reaching to pull the cookbook over when I set it on the kitchen island.

I grinned. It was sweet how Alfie continued to offer to chop things for me. Now that there was no time limit on our cooking, he could easily have left me to do it all myself. That wasn't Alfie's way, though, so he always wanted to help whatever way he could.

"That depends what you want to make," I answered. "I thought something fried might be good? I've been Googling why people don't like vegetables, and apparently, it's often because they've only ever had them boiled until there's no flavor or texture left in them."

I didn't want to accuse Alfie's nana of being a bad cook, but frying still seemed like it might be helpful. "And we can put in garlic or bacon, something to add extra flavor, too."

"Those sound like good suggestions," Alfie nodded. "Though, I'm pretty sure that garlic is a vegetable?" he joked.

Alfie did flick through the cookbook, scrunching his nose up at many of the images. I was starting to lose hope that he'd actually find something that looked appealing but then Alfie paused.

"This doesn't look awful," he decided, flipping the book around so I could look at the picture of deep-fried cauliflower. "It looks like chicken nuggets, maybe I can trick my brain into liking them."

I laughed at the idea of Alfie trying to trick his own brain, but nodded. "I've seen people use cauliflower for chicken wings, too," I said. "Maybe we can add a buffalo sauce for dipping."

It felt a lot like working together on *Serves You Right*, both of us contributing and building on one another's ideas. But this time, there were no cameras to worry about, and I was allowed to ask Alfie anything I wanted without anxiety that he wouldn't want the answer to be made public.

And I was allowed to kiss him, too, which I did before I set him up to chop the cauliflower into florets.

"Do you have any dreams for the future?" I asked as we started to work. I'd found out about Alfie's past, now I wanted to know what he hoped for going forward.

"Dreams?" Alfie repeated. "Like winning the Stanley Cup at least... I don't know, five times before I retire?" he joked. I shook my head at that. While hockey was not something I yet knew how to enjoy, even I knew that the Stanley Cup was a big thing. But that wasn't what my question had been about.

Alfie knew it, too, because he gave me a soft shove with his hip against mine. "I suppose I'd like to get married and have a family eventually. It's always been something I wanted, to have a family of my own."

My heart gave a leap for joy. It was too soon to be imagining Alfie and I having a family, but knowing it was possible, that it was something we both wanted, still thrilled something inside me.

"Yeah," I agreed, hoping that by sounding casual about it, I wouldn't risk scaring Alfie off. "That's something I want, too. Once I'm a bit more settled in my career, obviously."

And since we were talking about dreams... "I also think I might like to teach?" I admitted, my voice a little uncertain. "It wasn't something I was interested in before *Serves You Right*, but seeing you progress and learn about different foods has been really enjoyable."

Obviously, with Alfie, a big part of that had been getting to know him as a person. "I think I'd like it even if I weren't falling in love with the person," I added, nudging Alfie back.

The smile he gave me at that was so worth it. It seemed to light up the whole of his face and I had to remind Alfie to stop chopping before he lost a finger. He laughed, but did stop, setting the knife down so he could lean over and kiss me.

"As long as all your students don't fall in love with you," he teased. But then, his tone got a little more serious. "You would make such an excellent teacher. I've never cared about food before, I mean, I'm not sure I do too much now, but I definitely do a lot more than I did before meeting you."

Picking the knife up, Alfie waved at the cauliflower. "I'm even *floreting*," he informed me.

"You are," I agreed proudly. "You've done so well. And you really made me think about kids who didn't grow up watching the Food Network, and how they might still benefit from some lessons from someone who could get them a little interested in food."

How exactly I would go about reaching those kinds of kids, who I knew wouldn't necessarily have the money to pay for lessons, was something that I hadn't worked out yet. But this was all a dream for the future - I had plenty of time to iron out the details.

"And luckily, cooking's a skill that's always useful, no matter whether I stay in Salt Lake or not," I added. Alfie wasn't tied down to any one place, his job might take him all over the US, but I thought that I could work with that.

I smiled, holding out a spoonful of the sauce I was working on for Alfie to taste. "Spicy enough?" I asked.

He opened his mouth to let me give him a taste, before nodding. "Yeah," Alfie laughed. "I think that might be too spicy, if anything." Still, he'd let me offer him a taste. Alfie had come so far since that first day we'd met when he'd admitted that he didn't eat vegetables.

Now he was chopping up cauliflower for us to fry up.

"It's really cool that that's what you want to do, teaching kids how to cook. You've been so patient with me, I can easily imagine you teaching others. Do you think that's something you might use your winnings from *Serves You Right* for?"

It was a good question, and one which I'd been turning over in my head for the last week. It had been hard to completely come to a decision, because the truth was that I wanted to do both things.

"No, I don't think so," I said. "I think I'll stick with my original plan, set up a catering company. And then, maybe once that's established, see if I have time to teach as well. So I guess it's quite a long-term plan," I admitted. "And maybe things will change for me before I even do it. But it's good to have something to aim for, right?"

"It is good," Alfie agreed and then gave me another smile. "I'm very proud of you," he told me gently. "I know we haven't known each other a long time, but this competition... I've seen what a kind person you are, patient and caring. It's what made me fall in love with you."

Butterflies exploded in my stomach at his words. Alfie set down the knife again, turning to face me. "You're going to achieve all the things you want," he informed me, sounding so sure. "And I'm so excited to be there to watch it happen."

Without a moment's hesitation, I wrapped my arms around Alfie's neck, pressing my lips to his as if I could swallow up all his beautiful words and keep them inside me forever.

My heart did a somersault in my chest, my whole body seeming to blaze with joy. "And I'm excited to find out all the things we can't predict," I agreed as I pulled back. "No matter what happens in my life, I'm going to want you to be there."

Maybe I shouldn't have said that when we'd only been together for a week, but Alfie looked anything but scared. His face practically glowed with happiness. Knowing I'd been the one to cause it, I was sure my expression was nearly identical.

"I've loved every moment of *Serves You Right*," I said. "Apart from the skipping." That made Alfie laugh, no doubt remembering how much I'd struggled. "But you're still the best thing I got out of it. Even better than winning."

"You're the best thing I got out of it, too," Alfie told me. "And to think I didn't even want to do it..." He shook his head. I knew that if Alfie hadn't, there was no way we would have met. That wasn't something I wanted to think about.

So instead, we focused on the thing that had brought us together - food.

I showed Alfie how to make a batter for the cauliflower that we were going to fry. Like he'd been every week on the show, Alfie was quick to pick up how to do these things.

"You make it fun," he decided. "I don't just mean because I get to sneak kisses in, but just... you. You make cooking fun. No one's ever made cooking fun for me."

It made a pleasant warmth bubble in my chest, like the nicest bowl of hot soup on a freezing cold day. "I'm glad," I said softly. "Cooking is loads of fun for me, so it's good that I can share that with other people. I might never have known how much I enjoyed that if I hadn't come on the show."

But now that I did know it, I planned to do something with all that passion I had. Maybe not immediately, but in the future.

A future that I hoped would involve a lot more time with Alfie. It made me so happy to picture him in every moment - coming with me to restaurants, helping me plan my own menus for catering, playing games for the Pumas while I watched and cheered with Nadine. And, one day, maybe helping me to start that family we both wanted.

Whatever happened, I was going to welcome the future with open arms, secure in the knowledge that Alfie was the most supportive, generous, enthusiastic man I could ever hope to meet.

Epilogue

Alfie

The day the second season of *Served You Right* aired, Maya was catering a big event. She'd been buzzing about it for days. It wasn't the first event her new company was doing, but it was the biggest. So far, I had pointed that out and Maya had argued that if it didn't go well, she might never cater anything again.

Over the year that Maya and I had been dating, I had learned that Maya never grew more confident in her skills. But it seemed to help a lot when I encouraged her, so I tried to do that as much as I could.

She was achieving so much. Her company might have been set up with the winnings of *Serves You Right* but in less than a year, Maya was turning over an actual profit. At first, it had been just her and Sophie, but now Maya had another three employees.

The cooking lessons that she had wanted to do were also slowly coming together. Maya had a plan and Sloan, who ran our kids' hockey team, was helping Maya promote the lessons.

So many different things were going on that Maya was busy all the time. With my schedule, it didn't leave us a lot of time together. Which was exactly why Maya had moved in a few weeks back.

Even now, after two and a half weeks, my heart beat faster just knowing she was about to come home to me.

I heard Maya's car pull into the driveway and before long the door was being unlocked.

"Hey, you," I grinned, walking out into the hallway to meet her. She let me kiss her hello and take the boxes she was carrying through to the kitchen. That was one thing we reliably always now had - leftovers. "What unwanted things have you brought me tonight?" I teased.

Maya laughed, leaning against the counter to kick off her shoes. "I've brought Italian meatballs and garlic-marinated shrimp," she answered. "Which is a bit of an odd mix, but I thought I could serve one or other of them over some pasta."

She paused, eyes narrowing as she watched me pop a meatball straight into my mouth. "Assuming, of course, that you don't eat them all before I get a chance," she teased.

"I'm hardly going to let you cook for me when you've just spent a whole night catering an event," I pointed out. "Besides, even I can manage to boil some pasta." In fact, my cooking skills had improved hugely.

Maya cooked a lot for us, but she also let me help. But before Maya had moved in, I had plenty of evenings of cooking for myself. It hadn't become my favorite activity. Cooking was fine, though. Even if I still mostly avoided vegetables.

"Let me make you dinner tonight," I said. "And by that, I mean, I'll make the pasta and we'll microwave the stuff you brought home. That's the best bit anyway."

The smile Maya gave me was so soft and warm that it made my heart sprint against my ribs. I loved all the different ways Maya looked at me. It seemed as if there was a new one every week as our relationship got deeper and deeper.

I'd particularly enjoyed learning Maya's 'why are you waking me up with your noise so early in the morning?' look since we'd moved in together.

"But I like cooking for you," she said, her tone almost a whine. "It's way better than cooking for clients, even if it is just pasta."

I doubted Maya really meant that. She loved cooking for her clients, after all. But luckily for us, she could have both.

"And you must be tired, too, after training," she pointed out. "You should let me take care of you."

While Maya was right that I was a bit tired after training, we both knew that she was tired, too. It wasn't a battle Maya was going to win. Not tonight. Even if it was very difficult to say no to Maya.

"And you should let me take care of you," I pointed out. "How's your feet? Want me to rub them after dinner?" I was confident that that wasn't an offer that Maya could refuse easily. From the expression on her face, I'd clearly done well in suggesting it.

She sighed, settling down on one of the stools we'd added to my kitchen. Now that Maya had moved in, we both spent a lot more time here. Enough to justify extra seating.

"That would be lovely," she admitted. "They're not too bad, but they always feel so much better after you've worked your magic." It made me grin, pride swelling inside me. I loved looking after Maya and I knew she loved looking after me in return.

Watching me work, Maya smiled. "How was your day? Do you need anything iced?"

The question made me laugh. In the time we'd been dating, Maya had gotten pretty good at making hot and cold compresses for my injuries. Not that there had been many, but she worried even about bruises. It was... sweet. Having someone care for me like that? It felt good.

"No, nothing needs icing," I promised. Once the pasta was on, I got a couple of glasses, pouring us the leftover white wine. "Did everything go to plan? At the event?" I imagined that it must have, Maya probably would've led with it had it not.

"I think so," Maya said, which almost made me laugh before I saw how serious her face was. "No, I really mean it. Everything was so... busy," she explained. "It was honestly hard to process it all at once. You know you're better at that than I am."

It was true, hockey had given me an ability not to be flustered by a lot of different things happening all at once. Maya was getting better at it, especially when it came to watching the Pumas play, but I knew it wasn't as easy for her as it was for me.

"I'll know how it went tomorrow, once all that information has settled in my head," she told me confidently.

"But there were no big disasters!" Those words made her grin, as if she'd only just realized it herself.

"Well, we'll celebrate that," I announced, clinking my glass against hers lightly before pressing another kiss against Maya's lips. "And tomorrow, when you've thought about it, you can tell me all about it," I added. Listening to Maya talk about food and work hadn't become boring yet. The passion with which she spoke made me think that it never would.

Putting the meatballs and shrimp in two separate bowls, I put them in the microwave ready to be warmed up for when the pasta was almost done. While we waited, I reached for one of Maya's feet. The soft moan she gave as my fingers pressed into her soles was worth every second of my time.

"You do make such nice sounds," I teased.

Maya blushed, but she didn't object, just shifting her leg so she could press it against my thigh. "You make nice sounds, too, but those should probably wait until after we eat," she informed me.

That was fair enough. If we abandoned our dinner for the bedroom, we might never make it back. Maya was very particular about making sure I ate regularly, especially on days I had heavy training.

"Thank you for not being annoyed with me for how much time work is taking up," Maya added, looking very sincere. "I know it's hard right now, but it'll be worth it."

"Hey, hey," I shook my head. "We're a team, right?"

It was something I felt more and more confident in as every day passed. We'd worked together so well even the first day we'd met, but in the time since the competition, we had become an excellent team. Now that Maya and I lived together, that was especially apparent.

Things clicked together for us. I liked doing the sort of chores Maya didn't and vice versa. She did most of the cooking, but it seemed to bring her genuine pleasure. Especially when she convinced me to try something new, which was more often than me from a year ago could have ever imagined.

"Yeah," Maya agreed, wiggling her toes against me. "We're the best team." She smiled gently at me, then laughed before she added, "Well, apart from the Pumas, obviously."

I laughed too. The Pumas were doing well, even if we still hadn't won a Stanley Cup, but it felt very different from what Maya and I had.

"Obviously," I teased.

By the time the pasta was ready and the leftovers were reheated, Maya's feet were nicely massaged. I promised to do it again later, but only if she let us eat on the couch. Maya preferred for meals to be eaten at a table, said they tasted better, but sometimes, especially when we'd both had had a long day, we could snuggle up on the couch for dinner.

With the Food Network on, we ate our dinner, Maya's legs draped over my lap. "The pasta's really good," I informed her.

"I can see that by how quickly you're eating it," she teased me back. But from the contented look on her face, I knew she was pleased that I was enjoying myself.

Even with how fast I was eating, Maya finished before me. She put her bowl to one side, turning so she could snuggle against me and rest her head on my shoulder. "This is the best possible thing I could come home to after a long day," she said, happiness in every syllable. "I know it's only been a few weeks, but I love living with you."

Setting my own bowl down, I pressed a kiss against her forehead. "You're the best thing that comes home to me," I joked. "But yeah. I love it. I love you." Never had anyone felt like family the way Maya felt like family. With her food, and her tired feet, and her beautiful smiles, and her insistence that we watch nothing but Food Network.

"We really are the true winners of *Serves You Right*, I don't know how they'll top it this season."

Maya giggled, turning her head so she could press a kiss against my shoulder. "No, we got the best experience," she agreed. "But I think I'll enjoy watching what challenges they come up with. And it'll be even better if you watch it with me, because we can talk about what we would've done."

I gave a mock-groan. If Maya wanted us to talk about cooking, we could talk about cooking. She'd made a huge effort to learn about hockey so that she could both watch my matches and talk to the rest of the Pumas about how the season was going. It was only fair that I indulge her sometimes. Especially if we didn't have to actually cook after.

"I hope it keeps going," Maya added. "It's a good show, and it's great that the celebrity winnings go to such good causes."

"And it's especially good when the people in it get together," I joked. "I'm going to start a new #alfaya, see if it pushes them to find their best personal teammate ever."

Maya really was. My best personal teammate, my best personal team. She was the family I'd been looking for.

The Food Network would always be on in our house.

Salt Lake Pumas Series
Gloves Dropped

El Sterling ruined my life once. I'm not giving her a chance to do it a second time.

I've made mistakes.
Mistakes that I've learned from.
I've come a long way to make it as captain of the Salt Lake Pumas.

So of course, that's when *she* comes back.
The girl who ruined my life twelve years ago.

But not again.
I'm a changed man. I've worked hard for this.

My head knows I need to ignore the woman El has become.
My body's much more easily swayed.
The fire in her eyes burns through my cool-headed defenses.

No one told me that giving in to the sparks between us might make me change all over again.

A 68k standalone, enemies-to-lovers hockey romance!

Body Checked

Falling for a man who thinks romance is pointless is the stupidest thing I've done this year!

Everything happens for a reason.

The universe wouldn't bring a smart, sexy NHL player like Will Green into my life if we weren't supposed to connect.

Romance is more than just flowers and candy.
I'll prove it to him.

Except, Will doesn't *do* relationships.
Married to his NHL career, he told me that romance is a 'waste of time'!

That should be the end of it.

But destiny keeps bringing us together.
Even our *dogs* have formed a bond.

It has to mean something, and I will put my heart on the line to figure out what.

A 66k standalone hockey romance with a guaranteed happily ever after!

Penalty Counted

They say you should never fall in love with a bad boy. But what do you do when a bad boy falls in love with you?

I love to party.
Irresponsible, reckless and wild.
As a quickly rising star in the NHL, I can be whatever I want to be.

Meeting Morgan Acton changes all of that.
She is the bad girl to match my bad boy.

Our lust is instant, burning fast and strong.
But it's what comes after that stands the chance of ruining everything.

I shouldn't fall in love with her.

She's too intense to resist.
Her body calls to me and her recklessness makes me want to take that leap.

I might be a bad boy, but everything I know will be tested by her.
And I cannot wait.

A 69k standalone bad boy hockey romance with a twist!

Home Matched

Better to have loved and lost than never loved at all. Isn't that what they say? Why does nobody have advice for what happens when the love you lost walks right back into your life?

I was in love, once.
We were too young, too uncertain.
My NHL career wasn't compatible with her law school ambitions.

Promising to marry Helena Worth was the best decision I ever made.
And watching her walk away?
The biggest disappointment of my life.

Ten long years later, my brother is marrying Helena's best
friend.
A whole summer in our small town brings long lost feelings
crashing over me.

Falling back in love with my first girlfriend is a dangerous
game.

My love of hockey ruled my heart once.
Putting my career first again might break hers completely.

This summer will test everything I know.

About love.
About home.
And about myself.

**A 65k standalone second chance summer hockey
romance!**

Friend Locked

*Finding your perfect partner is a dancer's dream: a best
friend who moves to the same beat, who'll catch you every
time you fall.*

We met when we were ten.
From sharing a birthday, we quickly went to sharing
everything.
I couldn't imagine my life without Jessie Edwards in it.

I moved to Salt Lake City to join the NHL.
Being homesick for my best friend hit me hard.
But we learned to make it work.

When Jessie hurt herself dancing, there was no question that I would be the one to look after her.
But living together as adults was a dangerous idea...

Out of nowhere, my heart beat faster every time she smiled.
Sudden heat spread through me at a glance.

Sharing my feelings could cost us everything we've built together.
But not risking it feels just as frightening.

I could win her heart this winter.
Or break mine.

A 65k standalone friends-to-lovers hockey romance.
Best Played

Lying about having a date to my sister's wedding was a huge mistake. Convincing the NHL star I've had a crush on for years to pretend to be my boyfriend might just change everything.

I've watched him on the ice a hundred times.
I never dreamed he'd see me as anything more than a fan.
Getting close to Olle Sandström feels like a fantasy.

Because it is.
There's nothing real about the way Olle and I play happy families.
Every story is an act, every touch is just for show.

But we can't help being drawn together.
When we're alone, it feels far from a lie.

I've never wanted to be as honest as I do with him.

But the truth is never as simple as it seems.
When the past throws us challenges, we have to trust in each
other to get through them.

We are so good at faking it.
Now, I want us to make it.

A 64k standalone fake-relationship hockey romance.

Madison Howlers Series

Game Plan

Sometimes, knowing the name of your soulmate is more
trouble than it's worth. That's how Connor Lewis feels when
photographs of his soulmark get published.

The hockey fans go crazy. Every Ashley in the Madison area is
wild to convince Connor that she's the one. All Connor wants
to do is focus on his game.

Ashley Walton isn't looking for a soulmate. She wants a
relationship based on something real.

That makes her perfect for what Connor has planned. He asks
if she'll pretend to be his girlfriend, on the understanding that
it's just until the media frenzy dies down.

They expect it to be a few months, at most. Ashley's really
more interested in learning from the Howlers' PR team than
she is in Connor.

At least at first.

Everything about their 'relationship' is a show staged for the press. Except, Connor spends every waking moment with Ashley on the brain. Finding out she wants to move miles away for her dream job hits him like a body-slam into the boards.

The closer they get, the more Connor is willing to risk to keep Ashley at his side. Falling in love wasn't in their game plan, so Connor takes matters into his own hands...

Best Shot

Finding your soulmate is supposed to be *easy*! Especially when everyone carries their soulmate's name written on their skin.

Best friends Thea and Doe would never fall out over a man. Doe's soulmark reads 'Blake' and Thea's is 'Frederick', so the possibility has never crossed their minds.

Enter Blake Ashbury. Thea is first to meet the gorgeous hockey player. As soon as she finds out his name, she gives playing matchmaker her best shot. She should be over the moon to introduce Doe to her soulmate. It doesn't matter that Thea is the one who loves Blake's jokes, or that his touch feels like fire and electricity. Blake isn't meant to be with her, so Thea will back off.

At least, that's the plan.

Blake never expected meeting his soulmate to be so complicated. Doe is sweet. She's everything Blake thought he wanted in a girlfriend. He can't understand why it's Thea who makes his pulse race!

Thea and Blake aren't meant to be together, so *why* is it so hard to keep the chemistry between them down? The longer they spend together, the harder it becomes to remember that they need to keep their distance!

Empty Net

A tiny portion of the population have empty space where the name of their soulmark should be.

Ryan Newell believes that hockey is his one true love. Knowing he doesn't have a soulmate, he gives his heart to the Madison Howlers. It's only his *body* that he gives away freely.

A little too freely. A scandalous picture lands him in hot water with the team's PR. To fix his rep, they send him off to fundraise for a local charity.

That's where he meets Naomi Stone. Being blind since birth, Naomi has never *seen* the name that's written on her skin. All she knows is that Ryan makes her pulse race and her skin tingle in ways she's never felt before.

As things heat up between them, Ryan starts to feel like he's in over his head. Having a girlfriend isn't something you can *train* for. Knowing that he can't be Naomi's soulmate is a thought that Ryan can't escape.

Finding love is hard enough without knowing you are no one's destiny.

Goal Line

When your dad owns an NHL team, you meet a lot of hockey players.

Annie's daddy made her promise she'd never date one of the Green Bay Mammoths. That suited her just fine. Her interest was in their skills *on* the ice, not off.

But Devon Oakley changes everything.

Ever since she discovered the name of her soulmate, Annie has been waiting to meet him. And Devon's just as dedicated to his soulmark match as he is to his team.

But there's always a catch. Devon doesn't play for Green Bay. He's the goalie for their greatest rivals!

Annie has to know: is true love bigger than ice hockey loyalty?

There's only one way to find out...

Final Score

Finding a soulmate is different for everyone. Lev and I met at the side of the road and became friends over a common language. Then I had to tell him that I couldn't see him anymore.

Maria Rawlins is the best friend anyone could ask for.

Funny. Passionate. Twice shy.

Under her insistence that she doesn't need a man is a yearning for the kind of meant-to-be connection that her mom and sister have both found. She wants a Russian soulmate who loves life as much as she does.

A man who'll make time to be with her, who'll see her as his equal.

She doesn't notice Lev settling into the empty space in her heart. Not until there's no way to stop it.

A Russian-import NHL athlete, **Lev Popov** is...

Talented. Sexy. Wounded.

This devil-may-care extrovert could have any woman in Madison, but his heart is locked behind a wall built by his ex. Yet brick by brick, Maria is breaking it down.

Falling for his best friend is not what Lev wants. His heart races for Maria - and at the thought that loving her might mean losing her.

True love might be rare. True friendship can be rarer.